WARNING:
This book will self-destruct
if it falls into the wrong hands.
Make that paws. Rat paws.
(You know who you are.)

After being tipped off by an anonymous source (known only as 'Deep Rodent'), Heather Frederick knew what she had to do. She had to go undercover. She had to find out for herself the truth of what was happening beneath the floorboards.

Now she has broken cover to write books about the spy mice. 'The world needs to know the peril facing the brave members of the Spy Mice Agency,' she reports. She refuses to divulge her code name on the grounds that it would place her in danger. In addition, all the names in this book have been changed to protect active undercover rodent operatives.

Books by Heather Vogel Frederick

Spy Mice: The Black Paw

Spy Mice: For Your Paws Only

Heather Vogel Frederick

SPYMICE FOR YOUR PAWS ONLY

Illustrated by Adam Stower

PUFFIN

PUFFIN BOOKS

Published by the Penguin Group
Penguin Books Ltd, 80 Strand, London WC2R 0RL, England
Penguin Group (USA) Inc., 375 Hudson Street, New York, New York 10014, USA
Penguin Group (Canada), 90 Eglinton Avenue East, Suite 700,
Toronto, Ontario, Canada M4P 2Y3 (a division of Pearson Penguin Canada Inc.)
Penguin Ireland, 25 St Stephen's Green, Dublin 2, Ireland (a division of Penguin Books Ltd)
Penguin Group (Australia), 250 Camberwell Road, Camberwell, Victoria 3124, Australia
(a division of Pearson Australia Group Pty Ltd)
Penguin Books India Pvt Ltd, 11 Community Centre, Panchsheel Park, New Delhi – 110 017, India
Penguin Group (NZ), 67 Apollo Drive, Mairangi Bay, Auckland 1310, New Zealand
(a division of Pearson New Zealand Ltd)
Penguin Books (South Africa) (Pty) Ltd, 24 Sturdee Avenue, Rosebank,
Johannesburg 2196, South Africa

Penguin Books Ltd, Registered Offices: 80 Strand, London WC2R 0RL, England

penguin.com

First published in the USA by Simon & Schuster, Inc. 2005
First published in Great Britain in Puffin Books 2006
1

Text copyright © Heather Vogel Frederick, 2005
Illustrations copyright © Adam Stower, 2006
All rights reserved

The moral right of the author and illustrator has been asserted

Set in Baskerville MT
Typeset by Palimpsest Book Production Limited, Grangemouth, Stirlingshire
Made and printed in England by Clays Ltd, St Ives plc

British Library Cataloguing in Publication Data
A CIP catalogue record for this book is available from the British Library

ISBN-13: 978-0-141-31987-2
ISBN-10: 0-141-31987-9

For my true-blue family – Steve, Ian and Ben –
with happy memories of a New York City Thanksgiving

The Spy Mice Agency

The Rat Underworld

Scurvy

Gorgonzola

Stilton Piccadilly

Roquefort Dupont

Gnaw

The Limburger Twins

Brie de Sorbonne

CHAPTER ONE

DAY ONE – TUESDAY 0745 HOURS

'EEEEEEEEEYOWWWWWWWW!'

Something small and white catapulted across the upper corridor of the Library of Congress in Washington DC. If any humans had been present to witness the object's soaring flight, they would have been surprised to see that it was a mouse. A lab mouse, to be exact. But there were no humans present. Not this early in the morning.

The lab mouse turned a somersault and landed on the marble floor with a tiny thud. He lay there for a long moment, motionless. His skateboard – made from a lolly stick painted flamingo pink – lay upside down beside him, its wheels still spinning.

1

Finally, he sat up. 'It's no use, Glory,' he said sadly. 'I just can't do it.'

Another mouse stepped forward. A very elegant little mouse. Her glossy brown fur was impeccably groomed, and perched jauntily atop her head was a safety helmet crafted from a bottle cap and secured with a rubber band.

'Cheer up, Bunsen, it's not that bad,' she said, reaching out a paw and hauling her colleague upright. She began to brush him off vigorously. 'You're getting the hang of it. This is only the sixth time you've fallen this morning.'

'Seventh,' corrected Bunsen.

'So who's counting? You need more practice, that's all.'

'I've *been* practising day and night for weeks,' Bunsen moaned. 'Let's face it, Glory, I'm just not cut out for this. I should go back to work in the lab.'

'Nonsense,' said Glory crisply. 'Julius had good reason to promote you to field agent. Anyway, it's too late now. You've already graduated from spy school.'

'Barely,' muttered Bunsen.

'You just need to build up your confidence,' Glory continued, ignoring his glum face. 'Besides, all this practice is for a good cause, remember? Lives might depend on your skill some day.' She waved a paw at one of the many quotes that adorned the walls around them.

'I know, I know,' grumbled Bunsen. 'The Spy Mice Agency motto: *"The noblest motive is the public good"*. But what does some old Greek poet called Virgil know about skateboarding? I'll bet he never had to do anything like this in the line of duty.'

'I'll bet he wouldn't complain about it if he did,' chided Glory. 'You're getting your whiskers in a twist over nothing, Bunsen. You should have seen me when I first learned, and look at me now.'

Glory slapped her shiny silver skateboard – standard issue for elite field agents such as herself – down on to the marble floor. With a graceful leap, she landed on top of it, then pushed off with one hindpaw and flew down the corridor.

The tip of Bunsen's nose turned bright pink as he watched Glory carve her way down the long passageway. Beautiful, clever and brave, Morning Glory Goldenleaf was his work colleague, friend – and the mouse of his dreams. His eyes shone in admiration as she spun around, ollied up over a crack in the floor and slapped down on the other side, before whizzing to an expert stop in front of him.

'Perfect,' breathed Bunsen, gazing at her adoringly.

'Spin still needs work,' Glory replied, not catching his drift. She flipped her skateboard over and fiddled with one of its wheels. 'This back one still sticks, no matter how much I oil it.' She glanced up at her colleague. 'Come on, let me see you try again.'

Bunsen shook his head. 'I'm calling it quits for today,' he said, rubbing his sore behind. He picked up his skateboard – Glory's old one, on loan until he passed the agency's Basic Skills exam and earned an official board of his own. 'Besides, it's time we got a move on. The humans will be arriving soon and we don't want to risk being spotted.'

'You're right,' Glory agreed. 'Our rides should be here any minute, anyway.'

The two mice gathered up their gear and climbed on to the nearest window sill. A moment later, a gentle tap-tap on the pane announced the arrival of their Pigeon Air taxis.

'Right on time,' said Glory, wriggling through a crack under the sash on to the ledge outside. 'Morning, Hank! Morning, Ollie!'

The larger of the two birds bobbed his head. 'Morning, yourself,' he replied. As Glory started to climb on to his back, he added, 'Something you'd better see before we take off.'

'Can it wait?' she asked. 'We're on kind of a tight schedule. Julius will have my tail if I'm late again for the Tuesday morning staff meeting.'

'Trust me, Glory. You need to see this.'

Glory shrugged. 'OK.'

Once she and Bunsen were securely aboard, the birds spiralled upward towards the library's copper dome. All of Washington spread out beneath them in the steely November light. The wind was brisk, and Glory shivered.

The pigeons landed outside one of the dome's stained-glass windows, and the two mice slid off their backs.

'Take a look,' said Hank. 'The table nearest Father Time.'

Glory and Bunsen cupped their paws around their eyes and pressed their noses to the window. They peered at the library's magnificent Reading Room far below.

'There's no one there,' Glory reported.

'He's there all right,' said Hank. 'We spotted him earlier when we paused for a breather. Keep looking.'

'He?' Glory's heart skipped a beat. 'You mean –'

'Yep. I'd know that ugly snout anywhere.'

Glory peered through the window again, more urgently this time. She gasped. 'There! On the floor by the third desk from the end! Hank, you're right – it *is* him!'

'Roquefort Dupont, in the fur,' murmured Bunsen, eyeing the large grey rat with distaste. 'What on earth is he doing here?'

'And where has he been for the past month?' added Glory.

In the wake of his recent humiliating defeat at the paws of the Spy Mice Agency on Hallowe'en, the leader of Washington DC's rat underworld had vanished without a trace. Rumours of Dupont's whereabouts had circulated like wildfire, but for weeks now the mice had seen neither hide nor hair of him.

Glory and Bunsen watched as Dupont struggled to drag something out from underneath the desk. Something that looked suspiciously like –

'A book?' cried Glory in disbelief. 'Bunsen, is that really a *book*?'

'Impossible,' said Bunsen. 'Can't be.'

But it was. The two mice exchanged a glance. What could Roquefort Dupont, Lord of the Sewers and supreme commander of Washington's rodent forces, possibly want with a book?

'Maybe somebody accidentally smeared ketchup on it,' ventured Bunsen. 'Or used a sandwich as a bookmark.'

What other explanation could there be? Rats were as famous for their gluttony as they were for their contempt for the written word. Dupont and his kin were illiterate and proud of it. They had nothing but scorn for their mice rivals, who had forged a sophisticated society through shrewd use of human knowledge and technology. 'Not fit to be rodents!' the rats sneered, clinging stubbornly to their primitive ways.

'We've got to get in for a closer look,' Glory said. 'Hank, you and Ollie wait here. We won't be long. Come on, Bunsen.'

The two mice squeezed under the sash, emerging on to a deep plaster window sill. Bunsen crept cautiously forward and peered over the edge. He gulped. It was a long, long way down to the floor.

Glory rummaged in her backpack. 'Right tool for the right job, as Julius always says,' she said, pulling out what looked like a ballpoint pen. 'I've been wanting to test this.'

Bunsen inspected it closely. 'I see the lab's been

busy while I was at spy school,' he said. 'What kind of a range does it have?'

'Let's find out.' Resting the pen on her shoulder, Glory aimed it towards the stained-glass window behind them and sighted expertly along its barrel, then pulled the pocket-clip trigger. What looked like a shiny arrowhead (the nib of a discarded fountain pen, sharpened to a razor's edge) shot out, trailing a length of dental floss (foraged from a skip behind a dentist's surgery). The tiny harpoon arced across the sill, then buried itself silently in the wood of the window frame.

Glory nodded her approval. 'Now let's see how this floss performs.' The Spy Mice Agency had recently upgraded from yarn to reconditioned dental floss at the suggestion of Glory's brother Chip, who worked as a forager. Floss was sturdier than yarn, he'd argued, and easily come by at the city's many dentists. Less labour intensive, too. The yarn required for field operations involved many tedious mouse-hours unravelling discarded sweaters.

Glory tugged on the line of floss to make sure it was secure, and clipped it deftly through a karabiner (the metal tab from a cola can) on her utility belt (a discarded watch strap). She strode across the ledge and carefully and quietly lowered her harpoon pen towards the floor. Bunsen watched as the floss slowly unspooled. Lots and lots of floss. He closed his eyes and swallowed hard.

Glory looked at him. 'This is what we live for, Bunsen!' she said with a grin. 'You're a field agent now, remember?'

The lab mouse tugged unhappily at his ears. 'This field agent nearly flunked abseiling,' he confessed.

Glory gave him a comforting pat. 'Don't worry, you're in good paws. I won't let you fall. Wait here for my signal.'

Bunsen's stomach did a flip-flop as Glory leaped fearlessly off the ledge, hooked one paw around the line of floss and abseiled swiftly down, down, down the high wall. She landed on top of Father Time, whose statue adorned the fancy clock above the Reading Room's main entrance. Setting her backpack down, she gave the line a sharp tug to signal to Bunsen that it was his turn.

Reluctantly, Bunsen grabbed the dental floss with both paws – and wound his tail around it too for good measure – clipped it to his utility belt, then inched his way backwards off the ledge. His hindpaws waved wildly in the air for a moment as he eased into the first drop. He swung in towards the wall and would have crashed, but Glory held the line taut and he managed to steady himself. He pushed off and dropped again. Too fast! With a squeak of alarm, he toppled backwards and dangled upside down.

'Come on, Bunsen, you can do it!' Glory called softly.

With an effort, the lab mouse wiggled himself upright again. Hesitantly, he pushed off and dropped again, more successfully this time. Push, drop, push, drop – slowly at first and then faster as he found his rhythm. Finally, panting hard, he landed beside Glory. His pale face was flushed with pride. 'I did it!' he whispered excitedly.

Glory slapped him a high paw. 'Of course you did, Bunsen. You are true blue. It's like I said before, you just need to build up your confidence.'

She pulled a second ball of floss from her backpack and fastened one end to Father Time's sickle. 'Remind me to tell Chip that he was right – this floss works much better than yarn.' She dropped the ball over the side of the clock, waited for it to hit the floor, and abseiled the rest of the way down. Bunsen followed silently in her wake.

'We need to get close, but not too close,' whispered Glory. 'Dupont has a nose like a ferret.'

Camouflaging themselves in the shadows, the two mice edged nearer to where the grey rat was squatting on the floor. Dupont had the book in front of him now and was turning the pages with his mangy snout. Glory and Bunsen watched, speechless, as he squinted at the words, using his tail as a pointer.

'G-R-A-N-D,' he spelled, before slowly and laboriously sounding out the word. 'GRAND.' Dupont grunted. He sat back on his haunches. A look of surprise crept across his hideous face. He chuckled to himself. 'Well, whaddya know,' he muttered softly. 'The little beggar was right. It's not so hard.'

Glory and Bunsen looked at each other in horror. This was worse than they could possibly have imagined! Dupont didn't just have a book – Dupont was *reading*!

The power of the written word in the paws of a megalomani-rat like Roquefort Dupont? Glory's heart fluttered in fear. The prospect was terrifying. Books were the mice's secret weapon. Outsized, outclawed and outfanged, mice had no choice but to rely on brains rather than brawn when it came to dealing with Dupont and his kind. Reading gave them the power to do just that. It allowed them to retain a small edge over the rats, to stay a whisker's length ahead of their deadliest enemies. If the rats learned to read, it would tip the balance of power forever. Literate rats would be lethal rats. It would spell the end of civilization as they all knew it.

'Julius must be told at once,' Glory whispered. She turned to go.

Bunsen motioned her to stop. He slipped off his backpack and pulled out what looked like a small keychain. Slinging it around his pale neck, he held the black rubber key fob up to one pink eye and pointed it at Dupont.

'C-E-N-T-R-A-L,' the rat spelled, once again sounding out the word. 'CENTRAL.' He grinned, pleased with himself.

Click! Click! Click! went Bunsen's keychain. He looked over at Glory. 'Right tool for the right job, remember?' he said softly. 'Subminiature Tropel camera. CIA issue. No one will believe this unless they see it.'

Glory nodded, and the two mice melted back into the shadows. They retraced their steps, scampering swiftly up the trail of dental floss to the stained-glass window in the library's dome.

'Well?' asked Hank as they emerged into the open air.

'It's bad, Hank,' Glory replied grimly. 'Worse than bad – catastrophic. We need to get back to Central Command on the double.'

'What is it? What's wrong?' asked the pigeon.

Glory shivered. This time, it wasn't the November wind that sent a chill down to the tip of her tail. 'Dupont can read.'

CHAPTER TWO

DAY ONE – TUESDAY 0800 HOURS

Several miles across town, the morning bell rang at Chester B. Arthur Elementary School. Children streamed across the playground in response, heading for the building's back entrance.

'Watch it, Fatboy!' said a gangly sixth grader with a thatch of dark hair. He stepped heavily on the foot of a plump, moon-faced fifth grader whose wire-rimmed glasses partially concealed eyes as warm and brown as a golden retriever's. The moon-faced boy flinched, and his tormentor cackled with delight. 'Grab his lunch, Tank,' he ordered. 'Bet Oz's got something in there he's just dying to share with us.'

'Hey,' protested the fifth grader as the boy named

14

Tank snatched his lunch box away and started rummaging through it.

'Carrot sticks, an apple – Wait, what's this? – Score!' Tank waved a small plastic bag triumphantly in the air. 'Looks like cake.'

Pumpkin chocolate-chip bread, actually, thought Oz, gazing regretfully at his dessert. He had been looking forward to eating that.

Tank tossed the bag to his friend, then poked through the lunch box again. 'What's this?' he asked suspiciously, emerging with a neatly wrapped packet. He gave Oz a sharp poke.

'Uh, sushi,' Oz replied.

'Sushi?' Tank stared at it in disbelief. 'What kind of a loser brings *sushi* for lunch? Check it out, Jordan.'

Jordan sniffed the packet. 'Disgusting,' he said, then smiled. 'But it figures. I hear whales like raw fish.'

Oz stared miserably at his toes. It was starting again. Just like he'd known all along that it would. Oz was a realist, and he'd lived too long with sharks – his name for bottom feeders like Jordan Scott and Sherman 'Tank' Wilson, who lived to torture younger and weaker students like himself – not to expect the worst. Jordan and Tank had stayed off his back for a while following the Halloween incident, but recently they'd begun to rebound. Sharks always did. Oz knew this from bitter experience.

'Hold his arms, Tank,' Jordan ordered.

Tank obediently twisted Oz's arms behind his back and held them as Jordan unwrapped the packet of sushi and held a piece aloft. 'Feeding time at Sea World!' he crowed.

As a crowd of students gathered to watch, he crammed the sushi into Oz's mouth. Oz coughed and gagged.

'Whatsa matter, whale boy? Shrimp not fresh enough?' taunted Tank.

'Knock it off, you morons.'

Jordan and Tank swung around. A slender dark-skinned girl was standing behind them, a scowl on her sharply intelligent face.

'Should have guessed you'd come to the rescue, Dogbones,' Jordan sneered.

Dogbones – whose name was actually Delilah Bean, better known as DB – folded her arms across her chest and glared at him.

'Oooo, we are so scared!' squealed Tank in mock fear.

'You will be when Mrs Busby finds out what you're up to,' snapped DB. She pointed wordlessly to where their homeroom teacher was standing on the school's back steps. She'd spotted the commotion and was craning her neck to get a better view.

The sixth graders exchanged a glance. 'Here, keep your stupid lunch,' growled Jordan, dropping the sushi back into Oz's lunch box and thrusting it at him. Tank released his arms, and the two boys swaggered off, pushing the younger students out of their way as they went.

'Thanks, DB,' said Oz, wiping rice off his face.

'Any time,' his classmate replied. 'But, dude, you have got to learn to stick up for yourself.'

Oz sighed. 'I know,' he said. 'I'm trying. It's hard when they gang up on me.' Across the playground, a van pulled into the car park. 'Hey, isn't that your mom's film crew?' he said in surprise.

DB blinked, then nodded as Amelia Bean, ten o'clock news anchor and one of Washington's most famous faces, emerged from the Channel Twelve van. Spotting her daughter, she blew her a kiss. DB waved back reluctantly.

'What's she doing here?' Oz asked.

'Beats me,' DB replied.

A limousine pulled up behind the Channel Twelve van and the news crew sprang into action. Cameras

17

rolled as the rear door of the limo opened and a man emerged. He was dressed in a black suit like the Pilgrim Fathers wore, complete with square buckles on his belt and shoes and a tall black hat.

'Check out that clown,' said DB.

Another man got out of the limousine. A tall, bear-like man with a dark shaggy beard.

'Oh no,' said Oz weakly.

The man was followed by an equally large woman swathed in a purple kaftan. Her hair was the same pale blonde colour as Oz's.

'Aren't those your parents?' asked DB.

Oz scrunched down behind her in reply. His father was scanning the crowd of students, looking for him. 'Yeah,' he whispered.

Jordan and Tank materialized. *Like sharks scenting blood*, thought Oz, huddling lower. Jordan stared across the playground at Oz's parents, then lifted an eyebrow, causing the pimples on his forehead to scamper for cover in his greasy black fringe. 'Chip off the old block, aren't you?' he sniped nastily. 'Like mother, like son.'

Oz blushed. His mother was a world-famous opera star and, like many divas, she was amply proportioned. 'Larger than life,' his father always said admiringly. Fat, said the rest of the world.

Don't react, Oz told himself sternly. Reacting only fuelled the fire where sharks were concerned. He tried to imagine what James Bond would do if he were here. James Bond was Oz's hero. Agent 007 would never let a couple of thugs like Jordan and Tank rattle his cage. The British secret agent never let anything rattle his cage. Only problem was, Agent 007 didn't have parents. At least not that Oz knew about. And Oz knew pretty much everything there was to know about James Bond.

'The name is Levinson, Oz Levinson,' Oz muttered under his breath, trying to bolster his flagging confidence.

Across the playground, Oz's father shrugged, said something to Oz's mother, and ushered her into the school, along with the man in the pilgrim suit. Amelia Bean and her crew followed, cameras still rolling.

DB leaned over to Oz. 'Something's up,' she whispered.

'No kidding,' Oz whispered back. 'I wonder what?'

They didn't have to wait long for an answer. As soon as they had taken their seats in the homeroom Mrs Busby clapped her hands.

'Students! I have a surprise for you this morning,' she announced.

Here it comes, thought Oz, suddenly taking a keen interest in the surface of his desk. He scraped at an ink blot with his fingernail and almost – almost! – wished that he were invisible. Before Hallowe'en, Oz had spent a lot of time wishing he were invisible. He still didn't like being on the radar screen at school, and whatever his teacher's surprise was, it was going to involve him, Oz was sure of it. He glanced over at the desk next to him. DB was scowling. She didn't like being on the radar screen any more than he did.

'Ta da!' trumpeted Mrs Busby, flinging open the door to her classroom. The man in the pilgrim suit strode in, followed by Oz's parents and Amelia Bean and the Channel Twelve news crew. All of them were beaming.

'There you are, my little dumpling!' cried Luigi Levinson, waggling his fingers at his son.

A ripple of laughter spread across the classroom. Oz stared down at his desk again, his face burning. He could practically feel the bullseye spreading out on the back of his shirt. Jordan and Tank would lose no time making hay with that one.

'Oz, DB, would you please come up here?' said Mrs Busby.

Oz and DB exchanged a glance. DB lifted a skinny

shoulder in a half-shrug, rose from her seat and marched up to the front of the classroom. His face still red with embarrassment, Oz followed reluctantly.

'Roll 'em,' said Amelia Bean.

The camera's bright lights were hot, and Oz blinked in the glare. He started to sweat. His glasses crept slowly down his perspiring nose, and he prodded at them anxiously.

The man in the pilgrim suit stepped forward. He pulled a scroll of fake parchment paper from inside his coat, unrolled it, cleared his throat, and announced: 'Hear ye, hear ye! A Thanksgiving proclamation for Miss Delilah Bean and Mr Ozymandias Levinson from Mayflower Flour. *"Your ship always comes in when you bake with Mayflower Flour!"*'

He paused to let this brief commercial message sink in, then cleared his throat again and continued: 'Insomuch that your recipe for Pumpkin Chocolate-chip Bread has been tested and declared worthy, you are hereby declared finalists in the annual Mayflower Flour Bake-off, Junior Division!'

DB glared at Oz. 'You didn't tell me you entered us in a contest!' she hissed furiously.

'I didn't!' protested Oz, prodding at his glasses again. 'Honest!'

The two children looked at each other.

'Uh-oh,' said Oz.

They turned and looked at Oz's father. Luigi Levinson gave them an enthusiastic thumbs up. 'Surprise!' he cried.

'Terrific,' muttered DB.

Oz's heart sank. What had his dad gone and done now? A few weeks ago, he and DB had been messing around in the Levinsons' kitchen after school. Like his father, who managed the Spy City Cafe at Washington's International Spy Museum, Oz loved to cook. Almost as much as he loved to eat, in fact. He and DB had decided to make pumpkin bread to celebrate Oz's mother's return from Australia, where she had been on tour. At the last minute they had dumped in a bag of chocolate chips. Oz was a devoted fan of chocolate chips. He firmly believed that there were few dishes, with the possible exception of lasagne, that couldn't benefit from the addition of chocolate chips.

The experiment had turned out well. So well that Oz's dad had asked for the recipe and promptly added it to the cafe's autumn menu. But a contest? Not a word had been said about that.

The man in the pilgrim suit continued: 'Along with

eleven other finalists – a total of six in the adult division and six in the junior – you are hereby invited to the great city of New York, island of Manhattan, to compete in tomorrow's contest. You will be accompanied by parent chaperones and two lucky assistants.'

The classroom erupted in excited cheers. All except for Jordan and Tank, who were doubled over in laughter.

'Bet Pumpkinbutt looks cute in an apron!' jeered Jordan.

'Chef Blubber!' added Tank.

Oz stared miserably at his feet. No doubt about it, he was definitely back on the radar screen again. The sharks smelt blood, and they were beginning to circle. Soon, the feeding frenzy would begin.

Amelia Bean thrust a microphone under Oz's nose. 'What do you have to say, Oz? Is this a thrill?'

'Uh –'

'Do you know what the grand prize is?'

'Uh –'

Amelia Bean turned to her daughter. 'How about you, Delilah?'

'It's DB,' said DB, scowling.

Her mother sighed, then turned and faced the

camera. 'Grand prize in Mayflower Flour's Annual Bake-off Contest, Junior Division, is a five-thousand-dollar college fee savings bond, a year's supply of Mayflower Flour and a place of honour on Mayflower Flour's fabulous float in the Macy's Thanksgiving Day parade.'

'You *are* a float, Fatboy,' whispered Tank.

'Sherman, that's enough,' said Mrs Busby severely.

Amelia Bean looked directly into the camera. 'And now,' she said dramatically, 'the lucky finalists will choose the names of their two lucky assistants. Who will it be? Who will accompany them to tomorrow's bake-off in New York?'

Hands flew up all over the room. 'Me! Ooo, pick me! I want to go!' cried Oz and DB's classmates, waving wildly at them.

The man in the pilgrim suit swept his tall black hat from his head with a flourish. Mrs Busby dumped in it a pile of slips of paper containing her homeroom students' names. Oz scanned the room. *Tyler Chin,* he thought. *He'd be OK. And maybe Katie O'Keefe. Not friends, exactly. DB is my only real friend at school. But not sharks, either. Tyler and Katie are safe. They'd be good assistants.*

A hush fell over the classroom. Oz and DB each

plunged a hand into the pilgrim hat. They each plucked a slip of paper from the pile and held it aloft.

Oz prodded at his glasses with his other hand. He was breathing hard. The old familiar knot of panic had formed in the pit of his stomach. *Please, oh please,* he pleaded silently.

Mrs Busby took the slips of paper from them. She looked at them. She sighed a deep sigh.

'Well?' asked the man in the pilgrim suit.

The entire classroom stared at her expectantly. As the cameras continued to roll, Amelia Bean held out the microphone to catch her every word.

Mrs Busby forced a smile. 'Assisting Delilah Bean and Oz Levinson at this year's Mayflower Flour Bake-Off, Junior Division, and accompanying them to New York City, will be none other than . . . Jordan Scott and Sherman Wilson.'

Oz closed his eyes. Life as he knew it was over.

Jordan flashed him a malicious grin. 'You're mine, Fatboy,' he said. 'It's payback time.'

CHAPTER
THREE

DAY ONE – TUESDAY 0830 HOURS

The door to the conference room at Central Command burst open. Dozens of small heads swivelled around as Glory rushed in. Bunsen was right behind her, his helmet askew.

'You're late,' a stout grey mouse announced smugly.

Glory ignored him. Fumble was always trying to get her into trouble.

'We've got news,' she panted, unable to keep a tremor of fear from her voice. 'Bad news.'

The conference room buzzed with curiosity at this announcement.

Every employee of the Spy Mice Agency was required to attend the Tuesday morning staff meeting, and they had dutifully wedged themselves into a space that normally seated about a dozen. Field agents and foragers, computer gymnasts, surveillance pilots and lab mice – some standing, some leaning against the walls, some perched on spools and bottle corks and upended matchboxes and other bits of foraged furniture. Her colleagues looked at Glory expectantly.

'Well,' said Julius Folger, distinguished elder statesmouse and head of the Spy Mice Agency. 'What is it?'

'Dupont can read.'

The conference room went dead silent. No one breathed. Not a whisker moved. Every ear strained in Glory's direction; every bright little eye stared at her in disbelief. Julius blinked.

'What?' he said.

'Dupont can *read*,' Glory repeated, more urgently this time.

'Read? You mean, as in a book?' Her boss was clearly as stunned as his staff.

'Yes, Julius! A book!' Glory reached over and grabbed Bunsen. 'We both saw him just now at the

Library of Congress. So did Hank and Ollie. Bunsen even took pictures – isn't that right, Bunsen?'

The lab mouse nodded vigorously and held up his keychain camera.

The Spy Mice Agency director regarded them for what felt to Glory like an eternity. 'How the dickens did this happen?' he whispered, as if in a daze. Suddenly, he snapped to attention. 'This is a Code Red situation,' he announced crisply. '"For Your Paws Only".'

The gathered mice began whispering in excitement. Top secret!

'Everyone without "Paws Only" clearance will leave the room immediately and await further orders,' Julius continued, pausing to let the conference room clear. A trio of junior lab mice stood up and trooped out reluctantly. Fresh from their training with Kelvin Fahrenheit, Bunsen's uncle, at his laboratory in Baltimore, they were clearly disappointed to miss out on the classified portion of the meeting.

A whiff of something delicious – pumpkin chocolate-chip bread, perhaps? – wafted in as they opened the door to leave. Central Command was located directly beneath the Spy Museum's Spy City Cafe, and good smells often drifted down through the ventilation shaft. Glory's stomach rumbled. She hadn't eaten breakfast yet.

She watched as two apprentice foragers, a cluster of surveillance-pilot trainees and half a dozen computer gymnast students all trailed out after the lab mice.

'You too, Fumble,' said Julius, as the last mouse disappeared through the door.

Fumble, who had clearly been hoping that his boss would overlook him, reddened. He stood up and made his way sulkily through the crowded room. Glory waved cheerfully as he passed her, and Fumble glowered. He shut the door behind him with a resentful bang.

'If you'll take a seat, I'll begin,' said Julius. He waved Glory and Bunsen towards a pincushion sofa, which was only slightly less crowded now. The two of them managed to squeeze in next to Glory's brothers B-Nut and Chip.

'I don't know which news is worse,' said Dupont. 'Glory's, or this.' He held up a sheaf of paper scraps. 'The night-shift computer gymnasts just brought these emails in. London, Paris, Rome, Berlin – the news is the same from all corners of the globe. Rat leaders in nearly every major city have

29

been spotted stowing away on flights bound for New York.'

A hush fell over the room as the mice digested this information. Glory and Bunsen exchanged a glance.

'Julius, there's something else you should know,' said Glory.

'Yes?'

'Dupont might be heading to New York, too.'

Julius frowned. 'What makes you think that?'

'We heard him read two words,' Glory explained. 'Grand and central.'

'And I think they were in a guidebook for Manhattan,' Bunsen added soberly. 'I'm not one hundred per cent positive, but it's probably here on film.' He held up his camera again.

'Is that so,' said Julius softly. 'We'll need to get that developed right away.' He tapped his paw thoughtfully against the stack of emails. 'Something big is definitely up,' he continued. 'Something very big. This is a veritable rogue's gallery of rodents! Stilton Piccadilly from London! Brie de Sorbonne from Paris! Muenster Alexanderplatz from Berlin!'

'Not Muenster the Monster!' exclaimed one of the mice, as tails around the room began quivering in terror.

'I'm afraid so,' said Julius, nodding soberly. 'And it only gets worse – Gorgonzola himself was spotted creeping into the baggage hold of a plane in Rome last night.'

The conference room fell silent once again. Gorgonzola was a legend, as ruthless as Roquefort Dupont himself. Perhaps even more so, given the horrible rumours about his favourite food.

Julius stared morosely at the stack of emails in his paw. 'There's not a name on this list I'd look forward to tangling with. This is a crisis of enormous proportions. And now with Dupont able to read?' He shook his head and paced up and down in front of his staff. 'Word of this must not get out. If the press gets even a whiff of this – especially the *Tattletail* – it could create mass panic.'

Every head in the room nodded in sober agreement, imagining the uproar this news would cause throughout the tidy network of guilds that formed the backbone of their society.

'Above all, we musn't panic,' Julius continued. 'What's most needed are level heads. Calm, cool, clear thinking – that always wins the day. There is one bright spot,' he added, holding up one of the emails. 'Sir Edmund Hazelnut-Cadbury reports that

MICE-6 managed to smuggle two of their top agents on to the same flight that Stilton was seen boarding in London. They're hidden in a shipment of teapots and will rendezvous in New York with an elite team of our field agents.'

The elder mouse scanned the room. His gaze came to rest on Glory. 'I'm putting Morning Glory Goldenleaf in charge of that team.'

Glory's elegant little ears pricked up in surprise. 'Me?'

Julius nodded. 'I'm counting on your recent experience with rats – namely Roquefort Dupont – to provide just the edge we need here.'

'I'd like to take B-Nut and Bunsen with me,' said Glory. 'Hank, too, if you can spare him.'

'Very well,' Julius replied. 'And I'm recalling my nephew Hotspur from overseas as well, to join you.'

Glory and B-Nut exchanged a glance. Snotspur? She and her brother had gone to spy school with Julius's nephew. Like his uncle, Hotspur Folger was a member of the Library Guild. And not just any library, but Washington's Folger Shakespeare Library, one of the city's oldest and most distinguished families. Hotspur had graduated at the top of their class and quickly gone on to earn his Silver

Skateboard in record time. A good field agent, yes – but he was not exactly a team player. In fact, he was by all accounts a major pain in the tail. 'The mouse who puts the "do" in derring-do', he loved to call himself. Ambitious and arrogant, Hotspur craved the spotlight and the high life – fast skateboards and the fast track to the top. And rumour had it that he was not afraid to step on paws to get there. Glory didn't relish the thought of having to work with him, but Julius, unfortunately, seemed to have a blind spot where his nephew's faults were concerned.

'You'll need a cover story, of course,' added Julius. 'And it will have to be a good one. Again, word of this mission *must not leak out*. It's strictly "For Your Paws Only". We don't want to panic the guilds in New York or Washington. Or anywhere else, for that matter.'

'I've got the perfect cover,' offered B-Nut. 'If you'll give us permission to bring the Steel Acorns along as part of the team, that is.'

Julius raised an eyebrow at the mention of B-Nut's rock band. 'They're untested,' he cautioned. 'Greenest field agents we've got – well, besides Mr Burner, of course.'

Chagrined by this blunt assessment, Bunsen drooped slightly.

Julius paced back and forth, considering. He shook his head regretfully. 'I don't know about the Acorns,' he said. 'They're wet behind the ears. And they don't have "Paws Only" clearance.'

'I'd trust them with my life,' said B-Nut.

'Me too,' Glory agreed.

'Hmmm,' said Julius. 'Well, it's a bit unorthodox, but I think I see where you're heading with this, B-Nut. Might prove just the right tool for the right job. Let's get a move on, then,' he continued briskly. 'Computer gymnasts, find an empty keyboard upstairs and send out a worldwide alert. I want to keep our fellow intelligence agencies fully informed of every development.'

Worried murmurings arose from the computer gymnasts as, round-eyed, they looked at each other. Find a keyboard upstairs? In broad daylight? With the museum staff arriving even now? This was truly unprecedented, if Julius was going to risk allowing them to be spotted by humans.

As they filed out of the conference room, Julius continued barking orders.

'We need intel, and we need it fast,' he said. 'Lab

mice, get that film of Bunsen's developed on the double. I want it analysed yesterday. Surveillance pilots, I want you aloft in ten minutes. Not a tail moves in this city but you track it.'

B-Nut and the other pilots saluted smartly and followed the computer gymnasts out of the room. Julius turned to Bunsen. 'Mr Burner, you have my permission to take any equipment with you to New York that you may need. Deep Freeze is at your disposal. Chip, you and the rest of the Foragers assist him.'

The two mice nodded and hurried from the room. Glory started to follow, but Julius placed a paw on her shoulder. He waited until they were alone, then said, 'Given the nature of this crisis, I think it's time we called in our special agents.'

'Special agents?' Glory looked puzzled.

Julius nodded gravely. 'Contact the children,' he ordered. 'We're going to need their help.'

CHAPTER
FOUR

DAY ONE – TUESDAY 0850 HOURS

Roquefort Dupont, Lord of the Sewers and supreme leader of Washington DC's rat underworld, squeezed his hapless aide's throat in an iron-clawed grip. 'Gnaw, sometimes you just plain disappoint me,' he snarled, thrusting his face so close that their whiskers nearly intertwined.

Gnaw's close-set eyes bulged in terror. His lone ear (the other lost long ago in a brawl with Dupont) quivered frantically as he struggled to free himself from his boss's grip. He didn't know which was worse: having his air supply slowly cut off, or Dupont's breath. Fuelled by a steady supply of human garbage, his boss had the most rotten, rancid, repugnant breath of any rat in Washington. And Gnaw was getting a full blast of it.

'Sorry,' he managed to croak, his eyes watering.

Dupont let go. Gnaw fell to the floor with a thud.

'Your turn,' said Dupont, whipping around to where Scurvy, his other aide-de-camp, cowered beneath the desk in the Library of Congress's Reading Room. The skinny rat's droopy whiskers shook in terror as Dupont smacked the book that lay open between them with his long, hairless tail.

Scurvy peered at the page. His brow puckered apprehensively. 'Um, that's an N, right? And – wait, don't tell me! An E, and that's a W. Let's see, that spells, um . . .'

'NEW, Scurvy, NEW! As in NEW YORK! As in the BIG APPLE!' Dupont shook his head in disgust. 'Idiots! I'm surrounded by idiots!' he complained. 'I can see I'm just going to have to do this myself.'

Dupont's tail began to thrash back and forth angrily. 'Don't you two understand the importance of what I'm trying to do here? It's time to take this game of rat-and-mouse to a whole new level. It's time to finally take what we deserve! And the only way we're going to be able to do that is to beat those wretched small-paws at their own game.'

The rat leader's eyes gleamed fiery red in the shadows beneath the table. His aides drew back in alarm as their boss worked himself into a rage. 'It's time we rid the world of mice once and for all! And who better to do it than me, Roquefort Dupont?' He thumped his mangy grey chest with a powerful paw.

Gnaw began to chew anxiously on the tip of his tail. The boss was angry, and when the boss was angry, he took it out on his underlings.

Dupont stomped about beneath the desk. 'Rat scum, she called me! Me, Roquefort Dupont, the descendant of royalty! The great-great-great-great-great-great-great-great-great-great-great-great-great-grandson of Camembert Dupont, who lived in a castle! Well, I won't be insulted any longer! I won't be kept down, held back or pushed around. I will take my rightful place in this world, and she can't stop me!'

Gnaw and Scurvy exchanged a glance. Their boss was off again, ranting about Glory Goldenleaf. Ever since Hallowe'en, he had become increasingly unhinged. His hatred for mice – and for Glory in particular – had ballooned into an outright obsession.

'She thinks rats are ignorant,' Dupont fumed. 'Are we ignorant?'

Scurvy quailed. Gnaw pulled his tail out of his mouth cautiously. 'Uh, I dunno, Boss,' he replied. 'Are we?'

'Of course not, you useless garbage-trawler!' screamed Dupont. 'We're not ignorant, we're illiterate! Don't you know the difference?'

Gnaw blinked, confused.

'It means we can't READ!' Dupont thundered, thrusting his snout at him. Gnaw flinched, then popped his tail back into his mouth and began sucking it vigorously. 'But that's about to change,' continued his boss, a crafty look settling over his hideous face. 'Those wretched small-paws have a weak spot, you see. Just like that big human we saw in the movie – you know, that one in the cape and tights?'

'Spiderman?' Scurvy ventured.

'Not him, you idiot!' screeched Dupont. 'The other one!'

39

Gnaw pulled his tail out of his mouth again. 'Uh, Superman?'

'That's the one! Just like Superman. Kryptonite was his weakness. The short-tails have a weakness, too – words. If we can read, we can find out what makes them tick. Spy on their mouse plans, learn their mouse ways. And when we do? Well, you know what I always say.' Dupont's thin lips peeled back in a cruel smile. 'The only good mouse is a dead mouse. And the only world good enough for rats is a mice-free world!'

Dupont nodded in satisfaction at this thought. 'That Goldenleaf brat and the rest of her kind thought the Black Paw was bad. Wait until they get a taste of what I've got in store for them now.' He thumped his chest again. 'Me! Roquefort Dupont!'

There was a sharp creak as the door to the Reading Room opened. Dupont snapped his head around. 'Quick,' he ordered. 'Out of sight. No time to be tangling with humans. We've got a train to catch.'

And the trio of rats slunk off into the shadows.

CHAPTER
FIVE

DAY ONE – TUESDAY 1300 HOURS

'Hey, Oz.'

'Hey, Herbie,' Oz replied, waving at the Spy Museum security guard. DB waved, too.

'You kids are here earlier than usual,' Herbie noted. He frowned. 'Not cutting school, are you?'

'Nope,' said Oz. 'We got out early for the holiday weekend.' He sped through the lobby of the Spy Museum and headed for the hallway behind the Spy City Cafe.

'Where are you going?' called DB, trotting after him. She and Oz were a familiar sight at the museum. They hung out there nearly every afternoon after school, messing around in the exhibits, doing homework in the cafe and waiting for Oz's dad to finish work.

'Dead drop,' Oz replied.

DB looked surprised. 'Why bother? Glory can't help us this time, Oz. We're on our own. We're going to stupid New York, remember?'

'I don't care,' Oz said stubbornly. 'I'm going to leave her a note.'

He ducked down beneath the open grillework of the hallway's metal staircase and crouched in the shadows. The dead drop, located under the bottom step, was the place where he and DB and the Spy Mice Agency left messages for each other. Oz pulled a scrap of paper and a pencil from his pocket and began scribbling. DB peered over his shoulder.

'What are you going to tell her?'

'That we need help,' said Oz. 'That unless we come up with a plan, we are nothing but shark bait.'

He fished for the small roll of tape he'd stashed in the shadows and secured his note to the underside of the bottom step. He'd just finished when he heard a sound from the vicinity of his shoes. A very tiny sound, like somebody scraping their pinkie nail on a piece of sandpaper. Or like a mouse clearing her throat.

'Glory!' he cried in surprise, looking down to see

his friend perched on the toe of his trainer. 'What are you doing here?'

'Looking for you two,' Glory replied. 'This must be my lucky day – I was going to send you an email. Something's up, kids, something big. We need your help.'

'You think you need our help!' blurted DB. 'Oz's father entered us in some stupid contest, and we have to go to stupid New York tonight with stupid Jordan and Tank!'

Glory's ears pricked up at this piece of news. 'The Big Apple?' she said. 'Wait until Julius hears about this. Your trip might come in handy.'

'Handy?' snapped DB. 'Didn't you hear me? We have to go with *Jordan and Tank*.'

Ignoring her, Glory leaped gracefully off Oz's shoe. 'The thing is, Dupont has learned to read.'

'What?!' cried Oz and DB together, leaning towards their tiny friend so fast that they collided. They leaned back, gingerly rubbing their foreheads.

Glory nodded. 'Bunsen and I caught him in the act less than an hour ago at the Library of Congress.'

Oz and DB exchanged a glance. This was not good. Not good at all. They could imagine only too well what a thug like Dupont could do once he got his ugly snout into a book or two. Knowledge was power, and the last thing the mice needed was for the rats to gain more power than they already had.

'It gets worse, kids, believe it or not,' Glory continued soberly. 'We got word this morning that just about every rat who is anybody in the rat world is heading for New York even as we speak.'

'How?' asked Oz.

'Stowed away on international flights,' Glory explained. 'Rats say they don't have much use for humans, but they sure love eating human food and they sure love using human transportation. You should see the underside of the Metro trains at rush hour. They look like fur coats on wheels.'

'So what are you going to do?'

Glory shrugged. 'We don't know yet. I'm heading up a team to gather intelligence in New York. Once we know what the rats are planning, we'll report back and Julius will decide the plan from there. Meanwhile, I've been asked to recruit you two for a supply mission. Bunsen needs a few things.'

Oz reached into his pocket and pulled out the small gold button that he kept with him at all times. Julius had presented it to him just a few weeks ago when he'd made him and DB honorary Spy Mice Agency field agents. Glued to the back was a tiny safety pin; on the front, a pair of skilful paws had etched the Spy Mice Agency logo – the profile of a mouse in dark glasses.

Once again, Oz thought, *Glory's problems far outweigh mine.* As annoying as Jordan and Tank were, they were hardly lethal. Glory's world could collapse if Roquefort Dupont and the rest of the rat mafia harnessed the power of the written word. Oz squinted at the tiny line of script that circled the button's rim. He needed a magnifying glass to read it properly, but, no matter, he'd already memorized it by heart: *The noblest motive is the public good.* The Spy Mice Agency motto, from some old poet named Virgil.

'Mission accepted,' Oz said solemnly, pinning the button to his lapel. 'Agent Double-O-Levinson reporting for duty.'

Beside him, DB did the same. 'The only thing is,' she added, 'we leave for New York in a few hours.'

'So do we,' Glory replied.

'We'll have to move fast,' said Oz. He placed his hand on the floor, palm up.

Glory shouldered her mitten-thumb backpack and climbed aboard. She looked up at the two children and grinned. 'Well, then, what are we waiting for?'

CHAPTER
SIX

DAY ONE – TUESDAY 1345 HOURS

Oz was bulging with mice.

DB had had to bow out of the afternoon's mission. Her dad had arrived early to pick her up, and she'd gone home to pack. That left Oz to ferry Glory and her team upstairs all by himself.

'Hey, shove over, would you?' squeaked Tulip – better known as Lip – to Romeo, as the two Acorns jostled for more room.

Oz's colleagues had distributed themselves throughout his clothing: Glory and Bunsen were hidden in the pocket of his polo shirt, B-Nut and the Steel Acorns (Tulip, Nutmeg and Romeo) were spread out among his trouser pockets, and Julius was crouched under his baseball cap. He could feel tiny mice paws clinging to the fabric of his clothing, and the tickle of tiny whiskers and tails. It felt a bit odd, but it was comforting, too. He was literally covered with his friends.

'Dudes, keep still!' ordered B-Nut from the other side of Oz's trousers, as they entered the Code-breaking Exhibit. 'We don't want any humans to spot us.'

Giving a tour group from New Hampshire a wide berth, Oz slowly circled the large room. He passed the display on Navajo code-talkers, stopped briefly to examine the secret-code ashtray, then paused at Cryptology 101, where visitors could try their hand at deciphering coded messages.

Bunsen, who was squashed in beside Glory – and who obviously didn't mind, as not only his nose but also his entire tail was bright pink with pleasure – scanned the display cases that lined the exhibit. In one paw he clutched a tiny clipboard (made from a scrap of wood and a foraged hair clip), in the other, the stub of a pencil. The lab mouse was in his element, and fairly bristled with efficiency.

'See anything suitable, Mr Burner?' asked Julius.

'I would give my whiskers for a crack at that,'

Bunsen replied, gazing covetously at the glass case in front of them.

Number one on Bunsen's list of essential equipment was an encryption device. With Dupont now able to read, they couldn't risk having him intercept their messages.

'The soul of espionage is secrecy,' Julius had explained to Oz back downstairs. 'This mission must be strictly "For Your Paws Only". And that means mice paws, not rats.'

The Spy Mice Agency director nodded his grizzled head. 'The Enigma,' he said. 'Rightly so. It's the Cadillac of code machines. A real piece of history, too. Did you know that the Nazis invented it during World War Two, Oz?'

Oz nodded, and he felt Julius's tiny paws scrabble in his hair as he bounced up and down under his baseball cap. 'Thanks to the Polish secret service, the Allies got their hands on it,' the elder mouse continued. 'Helped turn the tide of the war. Operation Ultra, the humans called it.' He shook his head admiringly. 'They don't make them like the Enigma any more.'

Oz peered doubtfully at the machine, which looked like a huge, old-fashioned typewriter in a wooden box. Emphasis on huge. 'Uh, Julius,' he ventured, speaking quietly so as not to draw attention to himself. The group from New Hampshire had left, and they were alone in the room at the moment, but the museum security guards were never very far away. 'I don't think I can hide that in my suitcase.'

Once Julius had found out that he and DB were heading to New York for the bake-off, he'd enlisted them as mission couriers. Glory and her team would, of necessity, be travelling light, as pigeons couldn't pack much of a load for that long a flight. Oz and DB would transport the bulk of their equipment instead.

'No, no, of course not,' Julius agreed. 'It's far too big and heavy. We need something much smaller.'

Oz's clothing fell silent as the mice racked their brains for a solution.

'I have an idea,' said Oz. He ducked out through the Pearl Harbor exhibit and backtracked to the Secret History of History, the room devoted to the early evolution of espionage. Oz stopped in front of one of the display cases. He pointed to a round flat object about the size of a silver dollar. 'How about a cipher disk?' he suggested.

He felt his pockets wiggle as the mice angled for

a better view of the coin-like object, whose inner and outer rings were both rimmed with the letters of the alphabet. 'It's kind of an antique,' Oz admitted. 'They invented it during the Civil War. You just set the code by lining up any two letters of the alphabet. Simple stuff, but it might be OK, especially since Dupont's only just learned to read.'

Bunsen's pink eyes lit up. 'Oz, it's perfect!' he cried. 'A portable encryption device!'

'They sell them in the gift shop downstairs,' added Oz. 'You wouldn't even have to replicate them in the lab.'

'We'll need three,' said Bunsen, busily making a note on his clipboard. 'One for you and DB, one for our team and one to leave here at Central Command. Can you get them for us?'

Oz pulled his wallet from his pocket, being careful not to dislodge B-Nut and Nutmeg. 'I should have enough,' he said, looking inside. 'If not, my dad still owes me last week's allowance.'

'That's everything, then,' said Bunsen, scanning his clipboard a final time. 'I've got everything else we need back at Central Command.'

As Oz headed for the stairway that led to the

gift shop, Lip gave a low whistle. 'Dude, check out those cool shades!'

'Where?' Oz felt his pockets wiggle again. The wiggling stopped when the mice spotted the mannequin in a nearby display case. It was dressed in dark glasses and a trench coat.

'Video sunglasses!' said Romeo, reading the sign. 'Awesome!'

Bunsen tapped his clipboard smugly. 'Got it covered,' he reported. 'Retrieval mission brought them in just last week.'

'So are those phoney?' asked Oz curiously, pressing his nose against the display case.

'Yep,' said Bunsen. 'Lab did a good job, didn't they?'

Oz nodded. 'I sure can't tell the difference.'

Oz knew that at night, after the exhibits were closed, the museum turned into a virtual beehive of activity, as carefully coordinated spy mice missions got under way. Field agents like Glory and Bunsen scampered throughout the displays and offices, retrieving gadgets and whisking them down to Central Command. There, the lab mice crafted replicas from the foraged items, and the lookalikes were returned to the display cases before morning.

The humans weren't any the wiser, and the switch kept potential weapons out of rat paws.

'In fact,' Bunsen continued, 'I had the lab retrofit them with a bug. We'll have audio feed, too.'

'The better to see and hear you with, my dear, eh?' asked Julius.

'Exactly. By the time we're done with him, Dupont won't be able to twitch a whisker without us tracking it.'

After a brief stop in the gift shop, the expedition returned to the hallway behind the cafe. Julius made a very dignified leap on to Oz's palm, and Oz set him down carefully by the mousehole under the stairs. The other mice emerged from their hiding places in his clothing and scampered down his trouser legs.

'Everything we'll need for the mission is in here,' said Bunsen, patting an old lunch box (foraged from the museum's lost and found) adorned with a large purple dinosaur. It still carried a faint trace of that odour peculiar to lunch boxes, a combination of orange peel and wilted carrot sticks and peanut-butter-and-jam sandwich.

'Don't forget these,' said Oz, passing him two of the cipher disks. He pocketed the third.

'That's it, then,' said Julius. 'You're good to go.'

The mice lifted their paws in salute. Oz returned the salute, swallowing hard to hold back the lump in his throat.

'Good luck, Ozymandias!' said Julius. 'I'm sure the bake-off judges will find your pumpkin chocolate-chip bread irresistible. We certainly do. And thank you again for your help.'

'Any time,' Oz replied.

'Later, dude!' called the Acorns.

'See you in New York!' added Glory.

'See you!' said Oz, waving.

He watched as his tiny friends filed through the mousehole in the shadows that led down beneath to the Spy Mice Agency headquarters. How he longed to follow them! More than anything, maybe even more than wishing he could be James Bond, Oz wished he could visit Glory's world. He itched to see Central Command, and ride on a lolly-stick skateboard, and take a Pigeon Air taxi ride. He wanted to go out foraging with Glory's brother Chip, and take a tour of the lab where Bunsen and the other lab mice tinkered with their mouse-sized gadgets, and hear B-Nut and the Steel Acorns play at one of their rock band's gigs. Life would be so much easier in Glory's world, Oz was convinced of it. Everything was so small and tidy there. And, best of all, there weren't any sharks.

Then he remembered Roquefort Dupont. Oz shivered. No sharks, but there were definitely rats. Maybe life wasn't simple anywhere.

He picked up the equipment-filled lunch box and went to find his dad.

CHAPTER
SEVEN

DAY TWO – WEDNESDAY 0730 HOURS

The sky over Manhattan's East River was just beginning to lighten to a pearly grey as a small flock of pigeons circled the Rockefeller Center in New York. Far below, the city's streets were already jammed with cars and trucks and taxis, the pavements already thronged with humans hurrying to work. Not a soul looked up. Pigeons were a common sight in New York.

One by one, the birds dropped from the sky and landed on top of 30 Rockefeller Plaza. Glory slipped down off Ollie's back and blinked sleepily. They'd been flying all night, with only a couple of brief stops to stretch their legs.

'Nothing like taking the red-eye, eh, Sis?' asked her

brother. He yawned and dismounted from Hank, who tucked his head wearily under his wing and was fast asleep before B-Nut had finished unloading his gear.

Glory glanced around, drinking in the sights and sounds of the city. The honk-honk of morning rush-hour traffic floated upwards from the busy streets below and, a few streets to the south-west, she could make out the flashing neon billboards of Times Square. A rush of exhilaration flowed through her, and Glory's drowsiness fled. She was in New York!

'Where are we going now?' she asked her brother.

'You'll see,' B-Nut replied, shouldering his backpack. Out of the top of it stuck his lolly-stick skateboard and the neck of his guitar.

Glory sighed. Her brother was being frustratingly mysterious about this cover story he'd cooked up for them.

'This way,' said B-Nut, heading across the roof.

Glory, Bunsen and the Steel Acorns followed as he led them to a large vent. There, the mice paused to pull out their skateboards and adjust their bottle-cap safety helmets, then sped one by one down into the building's duct work. Bunsen, still wobbly, brought up the rear.

They emerged a few minutes later through a duct

under the sixty-fifth floor. Bunsen shot through last, landing with a crash. The others, who were used to this by now, ignored him. The mice peered around. The space was dimly lit, and Glory squinted at a darkened sign over the set of double doors facing them. '*BANANAS!*' it announced, the single word outlined in foraged Christmas-tree lights.

'Hey, I've heard of this place,' said Lip.

'Hoppingest club in all of Manhattan,' B-Nut replied with a grin. He opened the door and stepped inside. Glory and the other mice followed him into a cavernous, deserted room.

'Doesn't look very hopping,' Glory whispered to Bunsen. The room was dark and its floor completely bare. A jumble of furniture had been pushed against the walls – bottle-cork stools painted banana-leaf green, tables made from empty spools painted banana yellow and a couple of pincushion sofas covered in jungle-print fabric. The club's motif extended to the stage as well, which was flanked with pillars made from life-size plastic bananas.

Across the room, a lone grey mouse was sweeping the floor, whistling. B-Nut cleared his throat. The grey mouse looked up. His eyes widened.

'Well, if it isn't my old pal Banana-Nut Goldenleaf!'

he exclaimed, dropping his broom (a foraged make-up brush) and hustling over to them. A flashy gold chain circled his neck, from which hung an enormous letter 'B' encrusted with diamonds. 'Finally decided to take my advice and ditch that stodgy backwater you call home, did you?'

'Good to see you, too, Bananas,' said B-Nut, whose grin had broadened at the sight of the grey mouse. He extended a paw, and the mouse called Bananas shook it vigorously.

'Entertainment Guild,' Glory whispered to Bunsen, who nodded in agreement. The dramatic flair was unmistakable.

'Figured it was time to come to where the action is, did you? Hit the Big Apple? See the bright lights of Broadway?'

'Just for a few days,' B-Nut replied. 'Thought maybe you could squeeze my band in for a set or two while we're in town.'

'Are you kidding me?' Bananas crowed. 'The Steel Acorns? DC's hottest rock band? Wait until word hits the street. This'll really bring in the younger mice.' He rubbed his paws together in gleeful anticipation.

B-Nut turned to Glory and the others. 'Acorns,

meet my old pal Bananas Foster. He owns this joint.'

The spy mice nodded politely.

'This is Tulip, our lead guitar,' said B-Nut, pointing to a dark grey mouse who had slicked up the fur on top of his head into sharp spikes.

'It's *Lip*, man, just *Lip*,' Tulip whispered sulkily. 'How many times do I have to remind you?'

'Sorry, dude,' B-Nut whispered back. He turned back to Bananas. 'He likes to be called Lip. And Romeo here –' he slapped a paw on the shoulder of a big brown mouse who had shaved off all his fur except for a long ears-to-tail mohawk, dyed purple – 'is our bass player. Nutmeg, over there, is on drums.'

Nutmeg nodded a greeting. He was smaller and lighter in colour than the other Acorns, and he sported a black leather studded collar and a single hoop earring.

'Delighted, delighted,' said Bananas Foster, shaking paws with the three musicians. Turning his attention to Glory, he gave her a toothy smile. 'And who may I ask is this delectable creature?'

Bunsen's nose and tail turned pink in alarm as the nightclub owner reached out and drew Glory forward. The lab mouse stepped forward, too, taking up a protective position at her side.

'She's, uh, our lead singer,' B-Nut replied smoothly. Glory cast him a frantic glance, but her brother ignored her. 'Goes by the name of –' he hesitated for a fraction of a second – 'Cherry Jubilee.'

'Charmed, my dear Cherry, charmed,' murmured Bananas Foster. He bent over Glory's paw and kissed it. 'Consider me entirely at your service.'

Bunsen's nose deepened from pink to crimson. 'I'm the sound engineer,' he blurted, wedging himself between the nightclub owner and Glory.

Bananas Foster blinked at the lab mouse. B-Nut frowned. 'Uh, this is, uh –'

'Bunsen Burner,' said Bunsen firmly.

'Pleasure to meet you, I'm sure,' said Bananas Foster, craning his neck over the lab mouse's shoulder for another look at Glory.

'We're going to need a place to practise,' B-Nut said.

The nightclub owner prised himself reluctantly away from Glory. 'No problem,' he replied. 'Plenty of space backstage. Come on, I'll show you.'

'What's gotten into your brother?' said Bunsen, as the two mice moved off. 'For a minute there, I thought he was going to introduce me as Baked Alaska.'

Glory shook her head. 'All I know is our cover story just spun out of control.'

'What do you mean?'

'I can't sing!'

'Nonsense,' protested her colleague. 'You can do everything.'

'No, Bunsen,' Glory replied. 'I mean it. I really, truly can't sing. Not a note! I can't carry a tune in a paper bag.'

'Oh, dear.' Bunsen's forehead puckered with worry.

'What am I going to do?' Glory moaned. 'My first Silver Skateboard mission, and already things are going wrong.'

'We'll think of something,' Bunsen replied. 'Just play along, meanwhile.'

'What choice do I have?' Glory shouldered her backpack, and she and Bunsen followed the rest of the Acorns backstage. They found B-Nut and Bananas Foster in a large room whose walls were lined with foraged egg cartons.

'Look, Gl– I mean Cherry, soundproofing!' said B-Nut. 'This is perfect!'

'Perfect,' retorted his sister, flinging her backpack to the floor.

'Anything to make you happy, Cherry,' said Bananas Foster. He flashed Glory another toothy smile. The diamond-studded 'B' around his neck twinkled in the dim light. 'You need anything else, you just tell old Bananas and he'll get it for you in two shakes of a cat's tail.'

As Bunsen watched, scowling, Bananas Foster leaned over and kissed Glory's paw again, tossed her a wink for good measure, then left them to unpack.

'B-Nut, what were you thinking!' wailed Glory, the minute the nightclub owner was out of earshot. 'You know I can't sing!'

'What?' said B-Nut. 'I thought it was Blueberry who couldn't sing!'

Glory stamped her hindpaw in exasperation. 'You nitwit! My sister has a voice like an angel! I, on the other hand, sound like a swamp creature!'

'Well, you needn't get your whiskers in a twist. I can't help it if I'm feeling a little under pressure here!'

'Can't help it?' Glory cried. 'B-Nut, you're a professional! It's your job to help it!'

Bunsen and the Acorns moved hastily out of the way. It was no fun being caught in the middle of a Goldenleaf squabble.

'Uh, excuse me!' Bunsen squeaked hesitantly. 'I hate to interrupt, but I could use some help getting set up here.'

Glory glared at B-Nut and sighed. Bunsen was

right; they needed to focus on the mission. She'd deal with her lame-brained brother later.

'I'll need an hour or two to tap into the building's electrical and communication system,' Bunsen explained. 'And someone needs to locate a computer and let Julius know we've arrived safely.' He reached into his backpack and pulled out a pawful of tiny headsets (made from foraged mobile-phone parts). 'These will link us together for the mission. They're pre-set to the same frequency.'

Glory slapped her headset on and willed herself to snap out of her panic. 'I'll find a computer,' she said. 'B-Nut, you and the Acorns head over to Grand Central Station and keep a sharp lookout for rats. Report in if you see anything at all. We'll rendezvous back here when Hotspur and the British agents arrive.'

As the mice dispersed, Glory jammed her safety helmet on over her headset and picked up her skateboard. 'Cherry Jubilee indeed,' she muttered to herself, heading back to the ventilation duct. Bunsen had better come up with a plan soon. Otherwise, the minute she opened her mouth tonight onstage, their cover would be completely – and very publicly – blown.

CHAPTER
EIGHT

DAY TWO –
WEDNESDAY 0830 HOURS

'Glory?' Oz looked up from the bathroom sink at the Waldorf-Astoria Hotel in surprise at the sound of the gentle tap on the window. His tiny friend was perched on top of a pigeon on the ledge outside. Setting his toothbrush down, he wrestled the window open. 'How did you find me?'

'Easy,' said Glory, slipping off the bird's back. 'I used to be a computer gymnast, remember? I hacked into the hotel's reservation system and found your room number. Vinnie here did the rest.'

She motioned to the pigeon beside her, who lifted a leg in a jaunty salute.

'Uh, thanks, Vinnie,' said Oz. Leaning down, he whispered to Glory, 'I thought you said nobody was supposed to know about this mission. Top secret, "For Your Paws Only" and all that sort of thing.'

Glory patted his hand reassuringly, her soft little paw as light as a feather. 'It's OK, Oz. Vinnie works for us. He's Hank's cousin. Lives at the Bronx Zoo. Running Pigeon Air here in midtown is his cover.'

Vinnie winked at him, and Oz smiled in relief. 'I've got your stuff,' he said to Glory. 'I hid it in my suitcase under my pyjamas.'

A strange assortment of stuff it is, too, Oz thought. He and DB hadn't been able to resist sorting through the contents of the purple dinosaur lunch box last night when they'd arrived at the hotel. In addition to Bunsen's souped-up video sunglasses, there was a mobile phone (scratched and battered, it was much the worse for wear, but it boasted a small screen), a miniature tape recorder, a table-tennis ball, a book of matches, a magnifying glass and what looked like a kazoo. Oz couldn't imagine what Bunsen had in mind for all of it.

'Great,' said Glory. 'I knew we could count on you.'
'Where are the others?'
Glory rolled her eyes. 'B-Nut's cover for us is just a

few blocks away at the Rockefeller Center. A nightclub called *"BANANAS!"* under the floor of the Rainbow Room.' She shook her head and sighed deeply.

'What's the matter?'

'Oh, nothing for you to worry about,' said Glory. 'My absent-minded brother told the nightclub owner that I'm the lead singer. Only problem is – I can't sing. I mean *really* can't sing. He got me mixed up with our sister Blueberry. I've got a voice like a bullfrog with laryngitis.'

'Oh,' said Oz. 'That is a problem.'

'No kidding. Anyway, no point in worrying about it now. Our gig is hours away. What's your schedule look like today?'

Oz reached into the pocket of his bathrobe and pulled out a crumpled piece of paper. 'Uh, first bake-off session is from 9:00 to 10:30. I mean 0900 hours to 1030 hours. Then a half-hour break. From 1100 to 1330 hours, we're supposed to go on a tour of the Empire State Building and have lunch at Grand Central Station. The afternoon bake-off session is from 1400 hours to 1530.'

'Busy day,' said Glory. 'But lunch at Grand Central couldn't be better. We'll rendezvous with you there. Bring the equipment with you, OK?'

'How will I find you?' asked Oz, sounding worried again.

'Don't worry. We'll find you.' Reaching into her backpack, Glory pulled out a small scroll of paper and passed it to him.

'What's this?' asked Oz.

'Coded message. From Bunsen. He asked me to give it to you. Use pigeon post if you need to write back to him – or if you want to contact any of us, for that matter.'

Oz frowned. 'What's pigeon post?'

Vinnie stepped forward. 'One of my boys will be tailing you all day,' he explained. 'You need to get in touch? You just write your message, roll it up, step outside and hold it over your head.'

Oz grunted. 'Sounds simple enough.' He un-scrolled the tiny piece of paper and squinted at it.

'The magnifying glass in the bag is for you,' added Glory helpfully. She climbed back up on to Vinnie. 'Bunsen figured you'd need it.'

Vinnie flapped off into the air, and Oz poked his head out the window.

'Glory?' he called.

'Yes?' She tugged on the shoestring reins to make Vinnie circle back.

'What about the bake-off? Jordan and Tank have it in for me.'

Vinnie hovered in front of the window sill so that Oz and Glory were eye to eye. Glory regarded her human friend with concern. 'I know, Oz, but I can't spare anyone yet. Not until we've got a handle on Dupont and the other rats. Someone will be back to help out just as soon as possible, I promise. Hang in there meanwhile, OK?'

Oz nodded glumly. He'd been afraid she'd say that.

Glory saw the look on his face. She smiled at him. 'Come on now, Ozymandias Levinson. You're an honorary Spy Mice Agency field agent, and you're part of my team. You are true blue, and so am I. I won't let you down. See you at Grand Central!'

With a final wave, she and Vinnie flew off.

There was a knock on the bathroom door. Oz opened it a crack.

'For heaven's sake, Oz, what's taking you so long?' his mother asked. 'Hurry up now, sweetie! You have a busy day ahead, and you can't work on an empty stomach. DB and her mom are here already. Amelia and I are going to head down to breakfast. We'll save a spot for you two at the table.' She reached through the crack in the door and tousled her son's pale blond hair. 'I just know you and DB are going to win the bake-off! I can't wait to see the two of you up there on that float, riding in triumph!' Lavinia Levinson lifted her kaftan-draped arms dramatically upwards. As an opera diva, she did a lot of that kind of thing onstage. Offstage as well.

'OK, Mom,' said Oz. 'I'll be right out.'

He emerged a few minutes later, clean and dressed. 'Check this out,' he said, handing DB the scrap of paper from Bunsen. 'Coded message.'

DB brightened. 'Really? Cool.'

Oz rummaged through the lunch box for the magnifying glass and cipher disk. 'See those two letters?' he said, pointing to the 'N' and 'A' that Bunsen had written in bold across the top of the scrap of paper. 'That's the key to the code,' he explained. 'You line those letters up like this.' Oz twisted the cipher disk until the 'N' on the outside ring was lined up with the 'A' on the inside ring. 'Read me the rest of the letters and I'll tell you what they stand for.'

'SBE ... LBHE ... CNJF ... BAYL,' said DB.

Oz found the corresponding letters on the inner ring of the cipher disk and wrote them down. 'FOR YOUR PAWS ONLY,' he read aloud.

'Awesome!' said DB. 'It really works!' She continued to call out the letters and the decoded message soon emerged: 'GLORY IN TROUBLE. CAN'T SING. NEEDS YOUR HELP. SENDING SHEET MUSIC. HAVE DB USE TAPE RECORDER IN LUNCH BOX. NEED TAPE BACK BY 1900 HOURS.'

'He's sending music to me?' said DB, frowning. 'Why?'

Oz rummaged in the lunch box again and emerged with the miniature tape recorder. 'They've set up the mission command station in some nightclub called "*BANANAS!*" he explained. 'It's under the Rainbow Room at the Rockefeller Center.'

'I've heard of that place,' DB replied. 'The Rainbow Room, I mean. It's really fancy, right?'

Oz nodded. 'Anyway, Glory's undercover there with the Steel Acorns. She's billed as the lead singer. It was B-Nut's idea. The only problem is, he got her mixed up with his sister Blueberry. Glory can't carry a tune in a paper bag. She says she has a voice like a bullfrog. If she tries to sing tonight, she'll blow their cover.'

'Uh-oh,' said DB. 'That's not good. But I still don't understand – why would Bunsen send the music to me?'

Oz prodded his glasses, which had slipped down his nose as usual. 'Um,' he replied, 'I think he wants you to record the song. He's probably figured out some way for Glory to lip-sync it.'

DB stood up so fast she nearly knocked Oz over. 'Me? No way.'

'Why not?' said Oz.

'Glory thinks her voice is bad? I don't even sing in the *shower*. I'd probably scare the shampoo. And besides, even if I could sing, I can't read music.' DB folded her arms across her chest. 'No way, Oz.'

'Well, I certainly can't sing for her!' protested Oz. 'What are we going to do?'

He and DB stared morosely at the decoded note. Then they looked at each other. 'I guess there is somebody else we can try,' said Oz slowly.

DB relaxed her arms. 'Oh yeah,' she said with a relieved smile. '"It ain't over . . ."'

'"Until the fat lady sings",' finished Oz. 'We'll ask my mom.'

CHAPTER NINE

Roquefort Dupont crawled out from underneath the Metroliner train. 'New York, New York!' he crowed, stretching his legs and sniffing the air appreciatively. Doughnuts, pretzels, pizza, hot popcorn, bagels – the smells from the train station's many concession stands were mouth-watering, and Dupont's eyes glinted greedily. 'Now, this is my kind of town.'

Behind him, Scurvy and Gnaw emerged

from where they, too, had been clinging to the underside of the train. Limburger Lulu and Limburger Louie, Dupont's young rats-in-waiting, were right behind them, their eyes wide with astonishment.

Led by Dupont, the cluster of rats climbed cautiously up the side of the platform and poked their long noses over the edge. A herd of human feet clattered by, and someone trod on Scurvy's long, droopy whiskers.

'Hey, watch it, buddy!' he cried.

'Shut up, you fool!' snarled Dupont in a low tone. 'Do you want every human in the place to know we're here?' He gave his aide a vicious kick, and Scurvy went tumbling back down on to the track. He landed with a thud and clutched his tail, whimpering.

Dupont turned to his rats-in-waiting. 'So, kids, whaddya think? Was I right or what? Is Grand Central Station the rat's pyjamas?'

Limburger Lulu and Limburger Louie nodded enthusiastically in agreement. They always agreed with Dupont. That was their job. This time, however, they really meant it. Limburger Louie's stomach growled. It had been a long trip and he was hungry.

Dupont chuckled. New York always put him in a

good mood. 'I could use some breakfast too, Louie,' he said. 'And we certainly have our choice here. They don't call it the Big Apple for nothing. But first, we need to rendezvous with the others. We're meeting under Track Seventy-seven. Easy to remember, because there are seventy-seven of us.'

Taking one last look around, the rats crept back down and scuttled off into the shadows. Dupont, who as a ratling had spent many a vacation visiting his New York relatives, knew the city like the back of his paw. He led his aides expertly through the tunnels and duct work and pipes that connected the hallways and tracks, and within a short time they emerged at Track Seventy-seven.

'So where is everyone?' squeaked Lulu, looking around in disappointment.

'All in good time, my pet, all in good time,' said Dupont. He whipped his tail towards a grate on the far side. 'Watch for trains!'

With that warning, he darted across the track, shoved the sewer grating aside with a thrust of his powerful snout and disappeared through the hole behind. Scurvy, Gnaw and the Limburger twins followed close on his tail.

The rats descended into darkness, the twins

clutching each other's tails fearfully as they followed Dupont down, down, down into the bowels of Grand Central Station. The air soon grew close and warm, filled with the familiar, comforting scent of sewer water. Lulu and Louie breathed a sigh of relief. It was almost like home.

'Here we are,' announced Dupont, stepping out of the pipe into a large side-chamber of a sewer main. Dim light filtered down from somewhere far above, and the steady dripping of water echoed through the dark, dank space. The rats looked around to find that they were no longer alone.

'Roquefort! You made it! We were getting worried.' A beefy rat stepped forward and slapped Dupont heartily on the back. 'Good to see ya!'

'Uncle Mozzie, you old sewer-crawler, you!' growled Dupont, baring his sharp yellow fangs in a smile. 'How's Aunt Parmesan?'

'Feisty as ever. She sends her love. Says come over for some pasta if you've got time. There's this new restaurant down the street – you should see the stuff they throw out!'

'For that, I'll make the time,' replied Dupont. He turned to his aides. 'This here's my Uncle Mozzarella Canal, from right here in the Big Apple. Little Italy,

75

to be exact. Best skip diving in all of Manhattan –
if you like Italian food, that is.'

As Scurvy and Gnaw exchanged greetings with
Dupont's uncle, another rat stepped forward. A very
attractive rat.

'Roquefort, *mon cher*, how delightful eet eez to see
you again!' she murmured.

As Dupont's aides watched, their beady red
eyes popping in amazement, the sleek rat leaned
forward and kissed their boss on both cheeks.
Was Roquefort Dupont – Lord of the Sewers and
kingpin of Washington's rodent underworld –
actually *blushing*?

'The pleasure is all mine, Brie,' said Dupont, taking
one of her paws in his own and bending over it
gallantly to bestow his own kiss in return. He turned
to his speechless aides. 'May I present Brie de
Sorbonne, my cousin from Paris.'

Brie inclined her head regally at Scurvy and Gnaw,
who managed to stutter a greeting. Then she leaned
down for a closer look at the twins. 'Why, how utterly
charmant!' she cried, cradling their furry little faces in
her paws. 'Roquefort, you never told me zat you were
a father!'

Lulu and Louie's eyes grew round with

astonishment, and Dupont turned a brighter shade of red. 'Uh, well, no, I'm not, I've never – they're not mine, Brie. Just rats-in-waiting.'

Brie gave him a sly smile. 'Aha. So, *mon cousin*, zee fact is, you are still, how zey say – *available*?'

By now, Dupont was scarlet from the tip of his ugly snout to the tip of his ugly tail. Before he could speak again, however, a big rat with a powerful set of shoulders thrust himself between him and Brie. 'Enough of the pleasantries,' he said rudely. 'Time to get down to business.'

Dupont's upper lip curled, and he sniffed the air disdainfully. 'Stilton Piccadilly,' he snarled. 'I thought I smelt you. Since when do you call the shots around here?'

'Just because you called this meeting doesn't mean you get to run the show,' Stilton retorted. 'We're not your servants. Besides,' he continued, 'I didn't fly all the way from London for chit-chat. We've got work to do.'

Turning his back insolently on the British rat, Dupont surveyed the others. 'I don't know about the rest of you, but I need breakfast first,' he said. 'We can hardly be expected to conduct business on an empty stomach. How about it, rodents? Brie, a little *petit déjeuner*? And you there, Muenster – had anything to eat yet today?'

Muenster Alexanderplatz, a coal-black rat with a puckered scar alongside his snout, shook his head. '*Nein*,' he replied, his stomach chiming in with a loud growl.

A grizzled old rodent with a low-slung belly waddled slowly forward. As he did so, the other rats moved respectfully out of his way.

'Greetings, Gorgonzola,' said Dupont with a formal bow.

Gorgonzola inclined his head in response. The oldest rat in the group, he commanded respect both for his experience and his ferocity – not to mention his legendary appetite. An appetite that included . . . well, things most of his fellow rodents would never consider. Not even Dupont.

'*Si*, Dupont, you are right,' he rumbled, his low, raspy voice brushed with the lilt of his native Italy. 'We've travelled far. We need food *pronto* before we begin.'

There was a murmur of agreement from the others. Dupont shot Stilton a triumphant look. 'Seems you're overruled,' he said. Holding out a paw to his Parisian cousin, he inclined his head towards the sewer pipe. 'Shall we, my dear?'

As the rats filed back to the pipe that led up to Track Seventy-seven, they failed to notice the trio of small figures that hung suspended above them in the shadows.

'Greedy chaps, aren't they?' whispered one of them.

'You can always count on a rat to put his stomach first,' agreed another.

'"Glutton-like they feed, yet never filleth",' replied the third. 'To paraphrase the Bard, of course.' He began to climb paw over paw up a long strand of dental floss fixed to the sewer grate far above. 'You two stay here and keep a sharp lookout,' he called back over his shoulder. 'I'm going to find the others.'

CHAPTER
TEN

DAY TWO – WEDNESDAY 0900 HOURS

'I do not believe I have to wear this,' said DB, looking down at her apron in disgust. A beaming pilgrim standing on the deck of the *Mayflower* was plastered across the front, along with the slogan, '*Your ship always comes in when you bake with Mayflower Flour!*' 'This is worse than that stupid donkey suit we had to put on for Hallowe'en.'

She and Oz were standing on a platform in the Waldorf-Astoria Hotel's main ballroom. Behind them was a stove. In front of them was a work table. Five other identical platforms were placed around the edges of the room. On every one stood another junior bake-off finalist and their assistants, all of them decked out in Mayflower Flour aprons. The adult finalists were in the adjoining ballroom.

Oz looked over at DB. 'I know what you mean,' he replied. 'At least in the costume, nobody could see our faces.'

'Well, they certainly can't miss our faces now,' snapped DB. She pointed up at the giant TV screen that hung suspended above their work table. A camera on a tripod at the edge of the platform was trained on them, broadcasting their every movement to the crowd of attendees and judges that thronged the ballroom. Five other cameras and TV screens were positioned around the room to do the same for the other finalists.

'Is my head really that big?' DB complained, squinching up her face and watching as her TV self did the same.

Amelia Bean glanced over from where she stood talking with Oz's mother (outfitted today in another flowing kaftan; this one black, covered in constellations of sequinned swirls and loops). She looked up at the screen and frowned, then reached over to adjust one of her daughter's braids.

'Mo-om!' protested DB. 'This is a bake-off, not a beauty contest!'

Oz smothered a grin. DB's familiar fussing

somehow made him feel better. At least they were in this together. It would be a whole lot worse if he had to face the sharks alone. Still, he wished Glory would hurry up. He glanced over towards the door, wondering when she and the others would arrive.

The door opened just then, but instead of his tiny colleagues, Jordan and Tank entered the ballroom, reluctantly herded forward by their mothers. They, too, wore matching Mayflower Flour aprons. Jordan looked like he wanted to strangle someone, and Tank's face was as red as his hair.

'Shark alert!' Oz whispered, elbowing DB.

'Smile for the camera now, Shermie!' said Tank's mother, prodding him up on to the platform beside Oz. Tank grunted. Pretending to stumble, he stamped on Oz's foot.

'Ouch!' said Oz. 'What did you do that for?'

Tank, his back safely to his mother, glared at him. 'You're going to pay for this, Chef Blubber,' he whispered, tugging on his apron. He turned and grimaced at his mother.

'Good boy,' cooed Mrs Wilson, snapping a picture. 'All of you, now!'

Jordan stepped up reluctantly beside his classmates.

All four mothers whipped out their cameras to record the proud moment.

'AND NOW, LADIES AND GENTLEMAN!' came a voice over the loudspeaker. Every head in the room swivelled to see the man in the pilgrim suit standing at a podium in the far corner. 'FINALISTS, ARE YOU READY?'

Oz glanced down at the table. Flour, sugar, eggs, canned pumpkin, chocolate chips. He ticked off the ingredients mentally, then looked up and nodded at a judge who stood in front of them with a clipboard.

'LET THE TWENTY-FIFTH ANNUAL MAYFLOWER FLOUR BAKE-OFF BEGIN!' The man in the pilgrim suit banged a gavel down on the podium. The resulting crack was as loud as a gunshot, and Oz jumped. Loud music began pumping out of the speakers. The cameras zoomed in. Oz prodded at his glasses and went to work.

'Flour!' he called, and DB handed him the Mayflower bag. Oz measured out two cups expertly and dumped them into the bowl in front of him. He quickly fell into a comfortable rhythm as one by one he called for the ingredients and one by one DB handed them over. Cooking was as familiar to Oz as his own skin. Not that he'd ever let the sharks know that. They'd use it against him. Sharks always did.

He glanced over to where Jordan and Tank were standing, arms folded across their chests. They were scowling. He saw the judge look at them, too, shake his head and jot something down on his clipboard. Oz looked around the room. All the other assistants were busy helping. Like it or not, he had to get the sharks involved, or they'd lose the bake-off for sure. He turned to Jordan. 'I need two eggs,' he said. 'But they have to be beaten first. Think you can handle it?'

'Watch me,' smirked Jordan. He grabbed the egg carton away from DB, plucked out an egg and tossed it to Tank. Then he selected another for himself. Setting the carton down, he tossed the egg up and down casually, grinning at Tank.

Uh-oh, thought Oz.

The two boys started tossing their eggs to each other like miniature footballs. The camera followed their every move, and a crowd quickly gathered. They continued to toss the eggs, higher and further each time. The delighted crowd cheered at each successful catch. Slowly, inch by inch, Jordan and Tank moved closer to Oz.

'Such high spirits,' said Mrs Wilson. She snapped another photo of her son.

Lavinia Levinson looked up sharply, sensing trouble. Before she could intervene, however, the sharks moved in for the kill.

'Beat this,' sneered Jordan and, pretending to fumble the catch, he squashed both eggs against the back of Oz's head.

'EEEEEEWWWWW!' cried the crowd.

'EEEEEEWWWWW!' cried Oz. He recoiled as the broken shells released their warm liquid on to his neck. The egg yolks slid under the collar of his shirt and trickled slowly and disgustingly down his back. Oz squirmed, revolted. The judge frowned and made another notation on his clipboard.

'Bake-off Boy goes *down*!' cried Jordan, tucking his hands into his armpits and strutting across the platform in a triumphant chicken dance. Tank crowed like a rooster, and the crowd laughed.

Oz looked over at DB, who shook her head sadly. The morning was not off to a good start.

CHAPTER
ELEVEN

DAY TWO – WEDNESDAY 1015 HOURS

'Hit it, boys!' said Glory.

Nutmeg brought his toothpick drumsticks down on his cymbals (foraged soup-can lids) with a crash.

'One! Two! Three! Four!' he cried. And then, tail tapping behind him, head bopping to the vigorous beat, he launched into the spirited lead-in to the Steel Acorns' number-one hit, 'Born to Shake My Tail'.

The opening chords from Lip and Romeo's electric guitars (tongue depressors wired for sound) filled the small practice room. Bunsen winced, and his pale paws crept up towards his ears. B-Nut motioned to his fellow band members to lower the volume.

'Just enough to cover our voices,' he said.

Bananas Foster might be her brother's friend, but Glory was taking no chances of being overheard, soundproofing or no soundproofing. She didn't want anything to jeopardize the mission. Too much was at stake.

Before Glory could bring the meeting to order, the door to the practice room burst open and a tall, good-looking field mouse swaggered in.

'Let the party commence!' he cried.

Glory sighed. 'Hello, Hotspur,' she said without enthusiasm.

Bunsen watched in alarm as Hotspur looked Glory up and down and whistled appreciatively. 'Silver Skateboard status must agree with you, Morning Glory Goldenleaf,' he said. 'You are positively glowing. "Most radiant, exquisite, and unmatchable beauty", as the Bard would say.'

Glory sighed again. She'd forgotten Hotspur's habit of spouting Shakespeare.

Julius's nephew turned to B-Nut. 'Good to see you, too, dude,' he said. 'And these must be the Steel Acorns I've been hearing so much about.'

Without pausing in their strumming and drumming, Lip, Romeo and Nutmeg gave him polite nods.

Hotspur's eyes narrowed as he spotted Bunsen. 'Who are you?' he demanded.

'This is Bunsen, our newest field agent,' said Glory.

'Since when?' asked Hotspur rudely, casting a dubious glance at Bunsen's slim white form.

'Since Hallowe'en, when Julius promoted him.'

'My uncle promoted a *lab mouse* to field agent?' Hotspur replied with a sniff of disapproval. 'He must be losing it.' He reached out and squeezed Bunsen's slender bicep. 'You lab mice may have the brains, but you hardly have the brawn for this line of work.'

Bunsen's whiskers wilted at these withering words.

'Bunsen Burner is one of the bravest mice I know,' Glory retorted, rushing to her colleague's defence. 'Why, if it wasn't for him and B-Nut, my ears would have been nailed to Dupont's Wall of Trophies last month for sure.'

Hotspur shrugged. 'If you say so,' he said, unconvinced. He flexed his own bicep and gazed at it admiringly.

'Sit down, Hotspur,' said Glory sharply. 'We have

work to do. Where are the MICE-6 agents, by the way?'

'Bubble and Squeak?' Hotspur replied. 'I left them back at Grand Central. Figured it would be better to keep them on Piccadilly's tail.'

'But I specifically requested that everyone rendezvous here!' protested Glory.

'What difference does it make? We can bring them up to speed later.'

What difference did it make? thought Glory furiously. This was exactly what she'd been afraid of. Hotspur Folger was already throwing his weight around, trying to undermine her authority. If she didn't nip this in the bud, next thing she knew he'd be trying to take over the mission. Her mission.

'From now on, you follow orders,' she said sternly. 'My orders.'

'Whatever you say, Boss.' Hotspur yawned. 'Sorry, still a little jet-lagged. That red-eye's a killer. Of course, I should be used to it now, what with chasing rats across Europe.' He flashed them all a broad smile. 'London, Paris, Rome – it's a tough job, but someone's got to do it.'

Behind Hotspur's back, Glory caught her brother's eye. She grasped the tip of her tail in both paws and chomped on it in mock exasperation. B-Nut smothered a grin. Hotspur could always be counted on to brag about his exploits.

'Well, now that we're all here,' Glory began. 'Almost all of us, that is –' she glared at Hotspur, who smirked – 'I want to lay out our plan. You've got our electrical and communications systems up and running, right, Bunsen?'

'Except for the video feed,' Bunsen replied. 'There's a bug in the system I'm trying to sort out.'

'Keep at it,' said Glory. 'B-Nut, you and Hotspur and the Acorns and I are scheduled to rendezvous at noon in Grand Central with Oz and DB –'

'Who?' asked Hotspur, frowning. 'I don't recall any agents by those names.'

Glory gave him a speculative glance. Should she tell him about the children now, or let him find out for himself? She decided to let him find out for himself. A bit of a shock might do old Snotspur a world of good. 'You haven't met them yet,' she said simply. 'They're new. Julius hired them after you went overseas.'

She gave the rest of the group a conspiratorial wink, then continued briskly, 'Oz and DB are bringing the rest of the equipment with them and will make

90

the drop at lunchtime. Once everything's in place, we'll keep Dupont and the others under close surveillance. And when we have the intel Julius wants, we'll relay the information and await further orders.'

There was a knock on the door of the practice room. Bananas Foster poked his head in. 'Sounds good from out here,' he said. 'Catchy tune.' He held out a scroll of paper. 'Some pigeon stopped me on the roof just now and gave me this. Said it was for someone named Glory?'

Nutmeg, Romeo and Tulip automatically looked over at Glory. She froze. Julius was right – the Acorns were wet behind the ears. Experienced agents would never risk blowing her cover like that.

B-Nut jumped up and reached for the pigeon-post message. 'Ah, that's short for "Glorious Voice",' he said. 'That's what Cherry's fans call her.'

'Really?' said Bananas. 'Glorious Voice? Catchy. Can't wait to hear you tonight, Cherry.' He passed the scroll to B-Nut. 'Funny-looking writing. Almost like some sort of code.' He paused and added hastily, 'Not that I read it or anything.'

B-Nut chuckled. 'That Cherry Jubilee Fan Club!' he said smoothly. 'Always up to something. Must be trying out their new decoder rings.'

'I'll have to get one of those,' said Bananas, winking at Glory. 'Wouldn't want to miss out on any of the action.' He left, closing the door behind him.

'Sorry, Glory,' said Lip.

Glory shook her head. 'Don't worry about it. We all make mistakes. But thanks, B-Nut. That was quick thinking.'

B-Nut unscrolled the note, scanned it, and passed it to Glory. 'It's from Oz and DB by the looks of it.'

Bunsen scrabbled about in his backpack and emerged with the cipher disk. 'Fire away,' he called and, as Glory read out the sequence of letters, he twisted the outer dial into position, then scribbled the decoded message on to a tiny notepad.

'What does it say?' asked Glory.

'SHARK ATTACK UNDER WAY! SEND HELP!'

'Shark attack?' asked Hotspur, frowning again.

'No time to explain,' said Glory. She turned to the still-quietly-strumming Acorns. 'Boys, Oz and DB need you more than I do right now. Grab a pigeon – it's time to send in the cavalry.'

CHAPTER
TWELVE

DAY TWO – WEDNESDAY 1030 HOURS

Oz was back upstairs in his hotel room, changing his egg-soaked shirt.

'I can't understand why Jordan and Tank would do such a thing!' said his mother.

'Um,' said Oz, shooting a rueful glance at DB, who was sitting on the sofa. How did you explain sharks to parents? Before he could even try, there was a knock on the door and Amelia Bean poked her head in.

'You all about ready?' she asked. 'The tour bus is leaving in ten minutes.'

'I just need to wipe this stuff out of my hair,' Oz replied.

He went into the bathroom and had just begun

scrubbing the back of his head when a movement at the window caught his eye. A trio of pigeons were flapping off across Park Avenue and the Acorns were perched on the ledge. They waved.

'Hey, guys!' said Oz, opening the window. 'Am I glad to see you.'

'Tough morning?' asked Lip.

'Complete disaster,' moaned Oz. 'We're probably in last place.'

Romeo held out a scroll of paper.

'Glory's music?' Oz asked, and the bass guitarist nodded. 'Hang on a sec.'

Opening the bathroom door a crack, he beckoned to DB.

'What? Oh, hey, guys,' she said, spotting the Acorns.

Oz passed her the tiny sheets of music. 'Can you enlarge this? There's a photocopying machine by the lobby.'

'Done,' said DB. 'I'll meet you on the bus.'

'Wait!' squeaked Nutmeg. He opened his backpack and took out two human-sized headsets. 'Bunsen's upgraded our equipment. We're going wireless.' He handed them to Oz and DB. 'He says they should work just fine as long as you keep your CD player turned on, Oz. He's got us all preset to the same frequency.'

As DB headed for the lobby, Oz slipped on his headset and pocketed his Bunsenized CD player/transmitter. 'So what's the plan?'

The Acorns looked at each other and shrugged.

'Just go with the flow, dude,' said Lip.

'Go with the *flow*?' This was not exactly what Oz wanted to hear. 'These are *sharks*, Lip,' he explained. 'They don't exactly flow. They attack.' He held up his egg-stained shirt as proof.

'Don't worry, Oz, we've got it covered,' said Romeo. He puffed out his chest. 'We're official Spy Mice Agency field agents, remember?'

Oz chewed his lip. The Steel Acorns had been field agents exactly as long as he had, which wasn't very long. He sighed. 'OK, I'll do my best.'

Nutmeg stepped forward and leaped on to the toe of his shoe. 'That's the spirit,' he said. 'C'mon, dudes!'

With that, the three mice climbed swiftly up Oz's trouser leg and squeezed themselves into the pocket of his shirt. Oz looked down to see three pairs of bright little eyes looking up at him.

'Ready whenever you are,' said Lip.

'Our first solo mission!' added Romeo.

'Yeah!' cried Nutmeg, bouncing up and down beside him.

The mice's obvious excitement was infectious, and Oz felt his spirits lift for the first time all day. Maybe the happy-go-lucky Acorns didn't have a plan, and maybe they were no match for the sharks, but they were here and that meant he and DB were no longer alone. Oz smiled and shoved his glasses firmly on to the bridge of his nose.

'The name is Levinson. Oz Levinson,' he said in his best James Bond voice. 'It's time to rock and roll, dudes!'

CHAPTER
THIRTEEN

The dining concourse on the lower level of Grand Central Station was teeming with activity. Humans rushed to and fro, a constant flow that increased to a flood every few minutes as trains arrived. They thronged the counters of the numerous restaurants and snack bars, buying pizza and pasta, soup and sushi, cookies, cheesecake, tacos and more. Some of them took their meals with them, others claimed one of the many tables spread about the concourse.

'Where there's food, there's rats,' said Glory, and B-Nut and Hotspur nodded in agreement. The three of them were camouflaged inside one of the many

Thanksgiving holiday wreaths that hung on the train station's marble walls, watching all the hubbub below.

Like Oz and DB and the Acorns, Glory and B-Nut and Hotspur were also wearing headsets. In addition to being linked to each other, however, theirs were also linked to Bunsen, who was monitoring them from the command base backstage at *BANANAS!*.

'Any sign of rodent activity?' asked the lab mouse, his voice crackling through their earpieces.

'Not yet,' said B-Nut, who had a pair of miniature binoculars – originally attached to a keychain, the novelty item had been left behind in one of the booths at the Spy City Cafe, where the foragers had found it – trained on the floor below. 'Heck of a lot of humans, though.'

'You think this is busy, you should see Victoria Station in London. Or Stazione Termini in Rome,' said Hotspur.

Glory gritted her teeth. This mission was starting to get on her nerves. With any luck, they'd get the information they needed shortly and she could ditch Hotspur and his hot air and head back home. Glory could practically smell the Thanksgiving feast that her mother would already be busy preparing.

Glory allowed herself to daydream for a moment

of the holiday that would be celebrated tomorrow in the sturdy old oak tree that she called home. And what a celebration it would be! All sixteen of her siblings would be together for the first Goldenleaf gathering since their father's miraculous rescue last month. Her mother had planned an extra-special meal for the occasion. She would be in the kitchen right now, baking pies and rolls and –

'There he is,' said B-Nut tersely. 'By the rubbish bin across from the sushi counter.'

Jolted out of her happy reverie, Glory grabbed the binoculars from her brother. Fine Silver Skateboard agent she was, daydreaming when she should have been watching for Dupont.

'That's him all right,' she said.

'And that's Stilton Piccadilly right behind him,' said Hotspur.

'Whoa,' said Glory. 'He's a bruiser. Looks like he might actually be able to take on Dupont and win.' She passed the binoculars back to B-Nut.

Hotspur nodded. 'He's as nasty as he is big, too. Keeps London's guilds tied up in knots.'

'Speaking of London, where are Bubble and Squeak?' asked Glory. 'I thought you said you left them on Piccadilly's tail.'

'Uh-oh,' said B-Nut.

'What?' asked Glory.

Bunsen pointed towards the bin. 'Trouble,' he said. 'They're on Piccadilly's tail all right.'

Glory took the binoculars from B-Nut again. She gasped. Stilton Piccadilly was swishing his tail about with fierce glee. As he did so, two small mice swished with it. Bubble and Squeak were tied to its tip, and back and forth they went, scraping and bouncing over the hard marble floor in time to the hulking rat's cruel metronome. A cluster of other rats had gathered, including Dupont. They were all laughing.

Glory's stomach clenched. Mice torture was not a pretty sight. 'Right,' she said. 'I'm going in.' She drew the harpoon pen out of her backpack and assembled it swiftly. 'B-Nut, go back up on the roof and find Hank. Oz and DB should be arriving in the main concourse soon and someone has to be there at the rendezvous. We can't afford to miss them.'

'Got it,' said B-Nut. 'Be careful, Sis.' He scrambled up the wire that held the wreath to the wall and disappeared through a ventilation grate.

'Yes, Glory,' Bunsen's worried voice echoed in her headset. 'Watch your back!'

'Happy to watch it for her, mate,' Hotspur

chimed in.

This was greeted with silence from Bunsen.

Glory rolled her eyes and aimed her pen at a wreath a few metres down the wall. 'If we get the trajectory just right, we should be able to pull this off,' she said. Her bright little eyes narrowed as she calculated the distance between the wreath in which she was hidden, the one directly over Stilton Piccadilly and a third a little further down.

Glory glanced over at Hotspur. This was a dangerous manoeuvre, and she'd never teamed up with him before. Could she trust him, or was he just in it for the spotlight of fame? She'd couldn't risk any foolhardy heroics. There were lives at stake – spy mice lives. Still, two mice were definitely better than one for what she was about to attempt. It was a risk she'd have to take.

She pulled the trigger and her dental-floss harpoon soared across the wall. 'At least we'll have the element of surprise on our side.'

'Sometimes that's enough,' said Hotspur, pulling the trigger on his pen, too. His harpoon flew off, burying itself beside Glory's in the middle wreath.

'Nice shot,' said Glory.

'Think so? You should have seen me last September

101

in Moscow. I had to –'

'Not now, Hotspur,' said Glory, cutting him short. She plucked a small triangular blade from her backpack. It was a lapel knife, another World War Two invention designed to be hidden in the lapel of a uniform and used as a last resort in close combat. Humans held them between their thumb and forefinger, but they were just the right size for mouse paws and standard issue for Silver Skateboard agents. 'Ready?'

'Ready,' said Hotspur, holding up a blade of his own. 'Or, as the Bard says, "A rescue! A rescue!"'

The two mice clipped their twin lines of floss through the karabiners on their utility belts and leaped from the wreath. Down, down, down they dropped. The floss caught them just a few centimetres above the floor and they swung, Tarzan-style, directly at the cluster of rats.

Piccadilly had his back to them, his tail still slashing back and forth viciously. Moving in tandem, Glory and Hotspur swung boldly through the middle of the crowd. As they passed over Bubble and Squeak, they leaned down and simultaneously sliced through the lengths of twine that held their colleagues captive.

'Noon, upstairs!' Glory murmured in her target's

ear, and then up, up and away from the rats she swung. She and Hotspur swept like twin pendulums towards the third wreath, and as the two of them leaped into the greenery and reeled in their floss, Bubble and Squeak lost no time scampering to safety below.

'*Zut alors!*' cried Brie. 'What was zat?'

The rats gaped at each other in astonishment. They'd been caught completely off guard. They'd barely had time to register the sudden appearance of the two flying mice before they were gone again.

Dupont's red eyes narrowed. He lifted his snout and sniffed the air speculatively. 'An old enemy, if I'm not mistaken,' he replied. 'A Goldenleaf, to be exact.'

'Where are my mice!' shouted Piccadilly, whipping around to find nothing but twine attached to his tail. 'They took my mice!'

'She's too quick for you, obviously, old chap,' sneered Dupont. 'She didn't get away so fast last time she tangled with me.'

'Is that so?' sneered his British rival right back. 'As I recall, *old chap*, it was that very mouse and her friends who gave you a bath in the Potomac River last month. Unless the reports I happened to see on the telly were all wet.' He glanced around at the other rats and

103

chuckled at his lame pun. 'Get it? All *wet?*'

Enraged, Dupont lurched towards him, fangs bared. Mozzarella and Muenster rushed forward to intervene.

'Enough!' cried Mozzarella Canal. 'You're forgetting there are humans about. No point in risking the exterminator!'

'You stay out of my way or I'll exterminate you!' Dupont snarled at Piccadilly, as his uncle tugged him back into the shadows behind the rubbish bin.

'You owe me a pair of mice,' countered Stilton.

Up in the wreath above, Hotspur turned to Glory. 'You're good,' he said in surprise. 'Almost as good as me – although, of course, that's not possible.'

Glory couldn't help feeling pleased at the praise, however grudgingly given. She shrugged modestly. 'All in a day's work,' she said.

And leaving the rats to their quarrel below, the two mice headed for the rendezvous.

CHAPTER FOURTEEN

DAY TWO – WEDNESDAY 1130 HOURS

'Wow,' said Oz.

The view from the top of the Empire State Building was spectacular. The wind whipping around the eighty-sixth floor observation deck was cold, though, and Oz pulled his jacket closer as he and DB slowly circled the building.

'Brrrr,' said DB finally. 'I'm going inside.'

As she headed for the gift shop, Oz gazed out over downtown Manhattan. He spotted the Chrysler Building and Grand Central Station and, in the distance, the trees of Central Park. Far off to the south, on a small island in the harbour, a tall statue held her torch up proudly for all the world to see.

'Wow!' he exclaimed again. 'There's the Statue of Liberty!'

'Not fair! We want to see, too!' complained Lip over his wireless headset.

'Hang on, guys,' Oz replied softly. Keeping a wary eye on Jordan and Tank – the two sixth graders were busy seizing one of the deck's numerous telescopes from a fourth-grade bake-off finalist from Houston – he turned his back and unzipped his jacket slightly. 'The coast is clear,' he whispered.

Three furry little heads popped out of his shirt pocket.

'Awesome, dude!' cried Romeo. 'Just like the guidebooks said!'

The excited squeaks from the mice made Oz nervous. 'Pipe down, fellas,' he warned.

'Who're you talking to, Fatboy?'

Oz whirled around to see Jordan and Tank bearing down on him. As he did so, the Acorns' heads vanished back into his pocket. Oz clapped a protective hand over them, muffling the mice's chatter.

Tank poked him in the shoulder. Hard. 'He asked you a question!'

'Um,' said Oz. 'Nobody.' He drew his CD player from his jacket pocket and held it up, bopping his head to an imaginary beat. 'Just singing along, that's all.' He attempted a casual laugh, but it came out more like a bleat. *Levinson, you are pathetic!* he chided himself. He'd have to do better than that if he wanted to be a secret agent some day.

'Didn't sound like nobody.' Jordan's eyes narrowed suspiciously. He stared at Oz's pocket. 'What are you hiding in there?'

'Um,' said Oz, backing slowly away. 'Nothing.' Despite the chill wind, he was starting to sweat. He stopped, brought up short by the metal safety grille that topped the observation deck's wall.

'Keep your cool, dude,' whispered Nutmeg.

Oz forced himself to breathe normally. 'Nothing,' he repeated, more firmly this time. He glanced over Tank's shoulder, trying to hold back his rising panic. Where was DB? Couldn't she hear what was going on? He needed back-up, and he needed it now!

'Doesn't look like nothing,' said Jordan, moving closer. Oz tried to dodge him, but the sixth grader grabbed both of his arms and twisted them behind his back.

'Ow!' cried Oz. 'Let go!'

'Just as soon as we find out what you've got in your pocket.'

Jordan nodded to Tank, who stepped forward and reached out a beefy finger. He prodded Oz's pocket. The contents of the pocket wiggled. 'Hey!' said Tank. 'There's something moving in there!'

'Find out what it is,' ordered Jordan.

Tank cautiously inserted his finger into the pocket. 'It's furry,' he reported in surprise, poking around. The pocket emitted a squeak of alarm, and then – 'OW!' hollered Tank, pulling his finger back out and popping it into his mouth. 'Thumthing bit me!'

Oz's glasses had slipped down as usual and were in peril of falling off, but his hands were still firmly imprisoned behind his back and he couldn't reach them.

'Whatcha got in there, Blubberbutt?' Jordan demanded. 'A pet to keep you company? I'll bet it's a hamster. A fat one. Nice fat little pet for a fat little fifth-grade loser!'

'A hamthter!' wailed Tank, still sucking on his finger. 'I'll probably get rabieth!'

'We're gonna teach you – and your stupid pet – a lesson you'll never forget,' said Jordan.

He nodded to Tank, who lunged at Oz. Before he

could strike, Oz gave a desperate lurch and managed to wrench free of Jordan's grip. Shoving his enemy aside, he lumbered away, back towards where the rest of the bake-off finalists stood clustered around a tour guide.

Oz spotted DB threading her way to him through the crowd. Her voice came floating over his headset. 'I was buying postcards!' she cried. 'Sorry!'

'Code Red!' he called back. 'Gotta ditch the Acorns! Prepare for a hand-off!'

As he passed DB, Oz pretended to stumble and fall against her. 'Jump, dudes!' he ordered.

The Acorns leaped nimbly from Oz's pocket to DB's shoulder. Oz ran on. It was a bold move, neatly executed and, intent as they were on nabbing Oz, Jordan and Tank didn't notice the trio of mice. As the two boys thundered past, the Acorns scattered, hiding themselves in the profusion of small braids that crowned DB's head like a dark halo.

DB froze in her tracks. 'They're in my HAIR!' she whispered in astonishment, the wireless headset again picking up her words and relaying them to her colleagues.

'Don't panic,' panted Oz, as much to himself as to his classmate. The sharks – taller, slimmer and

109

much faster – were gaining on him.

'You're going down, Fatboy!' called Jordan.

Amelia Bean glanced over from where she was busily filming the view. She took one look at her daughter's red-faced, sweaty friend being hotly pursued by Jordan and Tank and hustled across the observation deck. Jordan and Tank screeched to a halt.

'What's going on here?' DB's mother demanded.

'*Ozymandias* brought a pet with him,' announced Jordan triumphantly. 'It bit Tank.'

Tank held up his wounded finger and adopted a sorrowful expression. His mother swooped down on him, clucking in alarm. 'Shermie! You're wounded!' she cried. She kissed the wounded finger and Tank turned beetroot red. 'My baby needs first aid! He might have rabies!'

Mrs Wilson whirled around to Oz. 'What were you thinking, bringing a pet with you on this trip, you horrid boy!'

Oz gaped at her. 'I don't own a pet,' he said. It was the truth. The Acorns were friends and colleagues, not pets.

'He's lying,' said Jordan. 'It's right there, in his pocket. A vicious hamster. Big fat one.'

Oz reached up and held his pocket open. Mrs Wilson peered in. So did DB's mother. 'Empty,' she said. 'Jordan Scott, are you making trouble again?'

'Again?' said Mrs Scott, rushing to her son's defence. 'My Jordan never makes trouble.'

'It's in one of his other pockets, then!' said Jordan, desperate to be believed. 'I swear, I saw it. It bit Tank!'

Tank held up his wounded finger again as proof.

Oz took off his jacket and handed it to Jordan's mother. She searched the pockets, but all she found was his CD player. Oz turned his trouser pockets inside out. He shrugged. 'See?' he said. 'No hamster.'

Jordan wasn't about to surrender so easily. 'He had a hamster, I swear it!' he repeated stubbornly.

Oz's mother appeared, accompanied by the Mayflower Flour man. He was still dressed as a pilgrim.

'Oz doesn't own a pet hamster.' Lavinia Levinson's voice was deep and imperious, and she looked every inch the diva in her flowing kaftan. She stared at Jordan. He swallowed hard and backed away. 'First the eggs, and now this?' she said. 'I'm beginning to think perhaps Amelia is right. Perhaps you are a troublemaker.'

Mrs Scott stepped forward. 'Now see here –' she huffed.

'Ladies, ladies,' said the Mayflower Flour man as the two mothers started to square off. 'I'm sure there's a reasonable explanation for this.'

Everyone looked at Oz. 'This was in my pocket,' he said calmly, holding up an open safety pin. 'When Tank reached in, he must have pricked his finger on it.'

'There, you see?' said the Mayflower Flour man, clearly relieved. 'It's all a simple misunderstanding.'

'Quick thinking, Oz!' cried Lip through the headset. 'You rock, dude!'

DB grinned and gave him a thumbs up. A small smile played on Oz's lips. *Now that's more like it, Levinson,* he congratulated himself. James Bond himself couldn't have done better.

Jordan and Tank glared at Oz. They didn't know exactly how, but they knew they'd been outfoxed.

Round one – sharks, thought Oz. *But round two most definitely went to the Spy Mice Agency.* The score was tied now, sharks against field agents. They were going to have to stay on their toes, though. There was more than one battle in a war. The sharks wouldn't give up. They never did, once they'd scented blood.

'Prepare yourselves, everyone,' Oz whispered into his headset. 'This isn't over yet. We're in for a fight.'

CHAPTER
FIFTEEN

DAY TWO – WEDNESDAY 1200 HOURS

'"What stars do spangle heaven with such beauty?"' quoted Hotspur, sweeping his paw towards the constellations painted on the sky-blue ceiling of Grand Central Station's main concourse.

'Let me guess,' said Glory. 'The Bard?' She glanced over at her brother and rolled her eyes. Between his bragging and the endless quotes from Shakespeare, Snotspur was really getting on her nerves. Some of the female mice fell for that sort of thing, but not Glory. She'd found it annoying back in spy school, and she still found it annoying now.

'There you are!' cried Hotspur, as two bedraggled mice limped around the corner of the marble stairs where Glory,

Hotspur and B-Nut were hiding. 'Meet Bubble Westminster and Squeak Savoy. Our counterparts from MICE-6.'

'Pleased to meet you,' said Bubble with a formal bow.

Glory cocked her head and regarded the sturdily built field mouse with bright little eyes. He reminded her a bit of Julius. Was it the bow tie? No, she decided, although Julius often wore one, too. It was the dignified air. *Church mouse*, she thought. With a name like Westminster, Bubble had to be from the Cathedral Guild. Quiet and aristocratic, church mice made excellent field agents, their placid exteriors concealing brave hearts and nerves of steel. Glory shook her new colleague's paw.

'Many thanks for saving our tails,' said Bubble.

Squeak Savoy extended her paw as well. She gave Glory a grateful smile. 'Stilton hit us from behind. We never saw him coming.' She shivered. 'For a while there, I thought – we both thought . . .' Her voice trailed off.

Glory patted her shoulder. 'I know the feeling,' she said. Even now, her stomach tightened, remembering Dupont's lair. She knew exactly what it felt like to think you were going to die, torn to shreds by your worst enemy.

'I could use a good strong cup of tea,' said Squeak, brushing at her pearly grey fur. It was matted with grime from being dragged across the floor of the train station.

Glory was surprised to see that her British colleague was a full-blooded house mouse. This was rare to find in a field agent – well, except for the Folgers, but they were a breed unto themselves. Most house mice were like Glory's own bakery-born-and-bred mother, gentle and home-loving, and tended to end up with rather sedate jobs. Until recently, Glory had been ashamed of her house-mouse heritage. She didn't want to be thought of as quiet and meek, and she certainly didn't want a boring job. She wanted a life of adventure, just like that of her father, the famous field-mouse general Dumbarton Goldenleaf.

Squeak noticed Glory inspecting her fur. She smiled again. 'Hotel Guild, both sides,' she said.

'Bakery Guild, my mother's side,' replied Glory, embarrassed that she'd been caught staring.

'You take after your father, though,' noted Squeak. 'As do you,' she added, with a nod at B-Nut.

'You've met him?' asked Glory's brother in surprise.

Squeak shook her head. 'We saw pictures in your family's file,' she explained. 'Sir Edmund Hazelnut-Cadbury briefed us thoroughly for this mission.' She swatted more dust off her soft grey fur. 'MICE-6 wasn't quite sure what to do with me at first,' she continued to Glory. 'So few of us house mice qualify as field agents. And Sir Edmund is quite traditional. But he couldn't ignore my track record – or the fact that I earned top marks in all our spy-school exams.'

Glory liked this feisty Brit. Squeak Savoy was definitely a kindred spirit. 'I'm afraid tea will have to wait,' she said, glancing regretfully at the large brass clock on the front of the concourse's information booth. 'It's noon, and Oz and DB will be here any minute.'

'How will we recognize them?' asked Bubble.

'Let's see, Oz is on the, um, plumpish side –'

'Fur colour?' asked Squeak.

'Pale for Oz, dark for DB,' Glory replied. Which wasn't too much of a fib, if you counted hair as fur.

'How about tails?' asked Hotspur. 'Long or short?'

'Um,' said Glory, stalling for time.

'There they are!' cried B-Nut.

Across the train station's enormous lobby, the Mayflower Flour man appeared, leading the bake-off finalists behind him. They followed him to the information booth, heads craned back as they looked up at the restored grandeur of the concourse's star-spattered ceiling.

'I don't see them,' said Hotspur, whipping his binoculars out and training them on the floor.

'You may want to aim a little higher,' said Glory, trying hard to suppress a smile.

Hotspur raised his binoculars a couple of centimetres. 'Tall, are they?' he barked. 'Must be field mice.'

'Not exactly,' said Glory.

Squeak caught on first. 'Do you mean to tell me –'

'You haven't –' said Bubble.

Glory nodded. 'For Your Paws Only,' she warned.

Hotspur put his binoculars down, clearly peeved that the others were in on something he wasn't. 'What are you talking about?'

Glory pointed to the group of junior bake-off finalists. 'The plump blond one with the glasses and the skinny brown girl with the dark braid thingies on her head.'

Hotspur's mouth fell open. '*Children?*' he croaked. 'The other agents are *humans?*'

Glory felt happy for the first time all day. It wasn't

often that old Snotspur lost his cool. 'Yessiree,' she said, smiling broadly. 'Human children. Fine agents, too, the both of them.'

'But Mouse Code forbids contact with humans!' protested Hotspur.

'No one else knows but us,' said Glory. 'Not even the Council. It's a Spy Mice Agency secret – strictly "Paws Only".'

Bubble and Squeak nodded and shrugged. The Americans always had done things a bit differently. Hotspur blinked, still trying to grasp this new development. 'Does my uncle know about this?' he said finally.

'He was the one who hired them,' Glory replied. She turned to B-Nut. 'You and Hank get ready. Wait for my signal.'

B-Nut nodded and sped away.

'But what – what –'

'Couriers,' said Glory. 'We couldn't manage all the equipment from Washington.'

'But – but –'

Glory laid a comforting paw on her colleague's shoulder. 'You'll get used to it.' She turned to Bubble and Squeak. 'Wait here until I return. Shouldn't be long.'

Glory drew her gleaming silver skateboard out of her backpack and stepped out of the shadows. She took a deep breath and furrowed her brow in concentration. She hadn't practised this next manoeuvre recently.

Placing the skateboard on the floor of the lobby, she waited until a human approached who was heading for the centre of the room. Then she leaped on to her board, got it rolling with a thrust of her hindpaw, and grabbed on to the turn-up of the man's trousers to hitch a ride. As he stepped forward, she released the turn-up and swung gracefully towards the other. Step, glide, step, glide. Her timing was flawless, and she quickly fell into a fluid rhythm. The manoeuvre was natural and effortless, and not a single human noticed the small mouse coasting across the room.

'Wow! That is wicked drafting,' said Squeak in admiration.

'Splendid pacing,' added Bubble. 'Absolutely tip-top.'

Even Hotspur had to admire Glory's skill. 'Couldn't have done it better myself,' he said grudgingly. 'Although there was one time, in Madrid –'

'Look! A flying ollie!' cried Squeak in excitement.

'I've never seen one executed on a live mission before!'

As her human ride veered around the group of bake-off finalists, Glory used the momentum of his stride to lift herself and her skateboard into the air. Detaching from his turn-up, she flew forward, landing lightly near where Oz was standing.

'Oh, well done,' said Bubble. 'Well done indeed.'

Hotspur didn't say a word.

Across the room, Glory returned her skateboard to her backpack and climbed nimbly up Oz's trouser leg to where his hand was tucked in a pocket. She patted it urgently with her paw.

Oz gave a start. He looked down. Glory waved. 'Hi, Oz!' she called softly.

Oz placed a protective hand over her and backed away slightly from the group. Jordan and Scott had been keeping a close eye on him since the Empire State Building. Moving his hand up to his face, he pretended to scratch his chin. 'Careful,' he said in a low voice. 'We're being watched.'

Glory peeked around his thumb. 'By whom?'

'Jordan and Tank,' Oz explained. 'They're suspicious. We had a little run-in a few minutes ago. But everything's under control.'

'That's good.' Glory sounded relieved. 'You

brought the merchandise, right?'

Oz pretended to scratch his nose. 'Yeah.'

'Be on the lookout for Hank and B-Nut. You'll be making the drop to them.'

'Got it.' Oz placed his hand back in the pocket, and Glory climbed down his trouser leg again, deftly retracing her steps.

'I wouldn't believe it if I hadn't seen it with my own eyes,' said Squeak as she whooshed to a stop by the stairway. 'That flying ollie was awesome. Can you teach me?'

'Sure,' Glory replied.

Hotspur sniffed and inspected the tip of his tail.

Bunsen's voice came crackling over their headsets, and the four mice sprang to attention. 'Vinnie and Ollie are in position on the roof,' he announced. 'The merchandise is heavy, Hank, but if you can get it to them, they'll help you fly it over here to the Rockefeller Center.'

'No problem,' Hank replied.

The mice watched as the Mayflower Flour group started to head for the hall leading to the food concourse.

'Now, B-Nut!' Glory called.

In a flash, her brother and his winged partner dived

for Oz. Oz saw him coming and motioned to DB, who pulled the purple dinosaur lunch box from under her jacket. She handed it to Oz.

'Whatsa matter, Fatboy, can't you wait until we get downstairs?' jeered Jordan.

'Looks like it's feeding time at Sea World again,' added Tank, moving to snatch the lunch box away.

As he passed DB, she calmly stuck out her foot and tripped him. Tank went sprawling on to the floor. Oz held the lunch box over his head and Hank swooped down, hooked his claws around the handle, and plucked it away from him.

'Hey!' said Jordan, as the bird wheeled upwards to the far corner of the ceiling, where a small hole led to the roof. 'Did you see that?'

'What?' said Tank, scrambling back on to his feet.

'That pigeon! It stole the lunch box!' Jordan said.

'What lunch box?' said Oz innocently. 'I didn't see a lunch box, did you, DB?'

DB shrugged and shook her head. 'First a hamster, now a lunch box. You two aren't just morons, you're nuts!'

And leaving the two sixth graders sputtering in frustration, Oz and DB turned and followed the tour group towards the food concourse.

'Brilliant,' said Squeak, watching from the safety of the stairs. 'Absolutely brilliant.'

'You were right, Glory,' added Bubble. 'The human children are a fine addition to the team.'

Hotspur sniffed again. 'You think that was brilliant?' he began. 'You should have seen me this one time in Stockholm –'

'Give it a rest, Hotspur,' said Glory with a grin. 'We've got work to do.'

CHAPTER
SIXTEEN

'You aren't worth your whiskers!' snarled Stilton Piccadilly, his red eyes blazing at Roquefort Dupont.

Dupont's tail thrashed angrily to and fro at this insult.

'How was I supposed to know that blasted Goldenleaf brat would show up?'

'Security would be tight, you promised!' Piccadilly continued, pacing back and forth across the sewer deep beneath Track Seventy-seven. 'Not a whisper will leak out, you promised! I sent a courier suggesting we meet in London, but no, you wouldn't have that. Everything had to be on your terms.' He leaned closer, sneering. 'Face it, Dupont, you're a joke. You don't have what it takes to cut it as Big Cheese. Now I, on the other hand –'

Dupont lunged. Piccadilly dodged to the side, and the two bull rats circled warily, the hackles of fur on the back of their thick necks rising in angry spikes. Before either could strike, Brie placed a restraining paw on her cousin's shoulder.

'Gentlemen, gentlemen,' said the she-rat in her silky voice. 'Zees is not ze time nor ze place for a duel. What happened was unfortunate, *oui*. Zose tiny short-tail spies might have given us much information, with ze right treatment.' She paused, licking her lips at the thought. Her eyes glinted in the dim light, revealing a hint of cruelty. Limburger Lulu and Limburger Louie drew back with a shiver. The lovely Brie had a darker side.

'Perhaps we can drop zis unfortunate business and get to work,' the she-rat continued. 'We have much to do before tonight.'

Dupont and Piccadilly eyed each other for a long moment, then grumblingly agreed.

Brie stepped up on to a half-submerged brick and began to address the assembled rodents. 'As Acting

Chair-rat of ze new Global Rodent Roundtable –'

'GRR!' chimed the gathered rats, baring their teeth in the agreed-upon response.

'GRR!' echoed Brie, then carried on briskly. 'I hereby declare zis meeting open. First order of business, induction of members.'

One by one, each of the seventy-seven rodents filed in front of their peers, their ugly snouts held high in pride.

'From Greece, Myzithra Moussikis,' announced Brie.

'Misery!' a rat in the back of the line shouted.

'From ze Nezerlands, Gouda Waterloo,' Brie continued. 'And from Spain, Zamorano de Castilla.'

As each new delegate was introduced, the rats gave the loud Global Rodent Roundtable 'GRR!' cheer. So busy were they with the introductions that not a single one noticed the four small figures descending slowly down the sides of the sewer vent above.

Glory motioned Hotspur, Bubble and Squeak to stop. 'Agents in place,' she whispered. The four of them hung suspended from long strands of dental floss.

Her headset crackled and Bunsen's voice floated across the airwaves. 'This is the dangerous part,' he said. 'You're going to have to get low enough to position the sunglasses properly. The minute you can see rats, stop. Be careful, OK?'

Glory glanced cautiously downwards. She knew only too well the stakes involved. A sewer full of rat kingpins, the biggest and baddest that the rodent world had to offer. All those sharp claws and jaws! Glory's heart began to beat faster, recalling her ordeal in Dupont's lair. Were they to be discovered – or worse, were one of them to fall – well, the end would not be pretty. It would be quite horrible, in fact. Dupont would have four new tails and four pairs of ears for his Wall of Trophies. If Gorgonzola didn't get them first.

She gave her colleagues a nod. Slowly, keeping a careful eye on each other to make sure they stayed in sync, the four mice gradually dropped lower and lower. Between them, strung across the vent on a web of dental floss, balanced the video sunglasses that Oz had brought from the Spy Museum.

Lower and lower the mice abseiled. Soon, they were able to make out dim shadows below. Another metre, and the rats themselves came into view. The fur on the back of Glory's neck prickled at the sight of all those long, hairless tails. She held up a paw and halted her descent. Her colleagues halted, too.

'OK, Bunsen, we've got them in view,' she whispered.

'Excellent. This is the tricky part, Glory. First, you'll need to secure the glasses.'

The four mice each removed a tack from their backpacks and silently inserted them into the mortar between the bricks of the sewer-vent's walls. When this was done, they expertly tied off the strands of dental floss that cradled the sunglasses. Glory tested the line with a paw. It held.

'Done,' she whispered.

'Now, one of you needs to climb out and flip the switch,' said Bunsen.

'I'll go.' Glory inched her way out on to the web of floss. As nearly weightless as she was, the tightrope-like strands still dipped and swayed with each step. She gulped but didn't look down, fixing her gaze instead on the target – the black sunglasses, their lenses pointed directly at the cluster of rats below.

'What was that?' cried Dupont.

Glory froze, teetering on the floss. Her heart pattered wildly. She'd been spotted!

'What did you say his name was?' repeated Dupont.

'Havarti Lergravsparken,' said Brie. 'From Copenhagen.'

Glory breathed a sigh of relief. Dupont hadn't seen her after all. He was still busy admitting rats into the – what had Brie called it? – the Global Rodent Roundtable?

She crept forward, stopping when she reached the sunglasses. Reaching out a careful paw, she flipped the tiny switch camouflaged by a screw in the frames.

'OK, Bunsen,' she whispered. 'They're on.'

'We have lift-off!' her colleague squeaked excitedly in her ear. 'Can you angle the video camera a little more to the left?'

Glory fiddled with the sunglasses.

'Perfect!' said Bunsen. 'The pigeons are waiting for you on the roof.'

And just as silently as they had appeared, the four mice vanished into the shadows.

CHAPTER
SEVENTEEN

'This isn't over yet,' said Tank.

'Not by a long shot,' added Jordan.

Oz glanced warily at the sixth graders. They were smiling for the TV camera in the Waldorf-Astoria's ballroom, their faces the picture of sunshine and innocence. The afternoon bake-off session was about to get under way.

Oz frowned. After the disastrous morning session, he didn't hold out too much hope for the contest's outcome. He stared ruefully at the failed loaf of pumpkin bread that squatted on the edge of his work table. It looked like a squashed brick. The eggs Jordan had smashed against his neck had broken his concentration, and he'd forgotten to add the baking powder. 'Sixth place' read the card propped on the

131

plate. Dead last. *Pathetic,* thought Oz glumly. *What a loser.*

He desperately didn't want to be a loser. Especially not when it involved something he was actually good at, like cooking. Oz didn't want to come in last. Not in front of Jordan and Tank. It would be just too humiliating.

The Mayflower Flour man banged his gavel and Oz picked up the bag of flour, keeping a sharp eye on the sharks. His classmates grinned at him.

'Can I give you a hand there, Oz?' asked Jordan jovially.

'Here, let me help.' Tank whipped out a measuring cup, the very picture of politeness. Both boys smiled for the camera. 'There you go, Oz!'

'Exemplary teamwork,' said one of the watching judges, checking something off on his clipboard. 'Extra points.'

'Sugar, Oz?' asked Jordan, practically bowing as he rushed forward with another measuring cup.

Oz and DB exchanged a glance. The unexpected politeness was unnerving.

'I think I like it better when they act like sharks,' whispered DB.

'I know what you mean,' Oz whispered back.

'At least then we know what to expect.'

One after another, the ingredients were transferred smoothly into the mixing bowl. Jordan and Tank scuttled about like a pair of reformed convicts, beaming at Oz, beaming at DB, beaming at the camera.

'See?' said Mrs Scott to Mrs Wilson in a loud stage whisper, for Lavinia Levinson and Amelia Bean's benefit. 'My Jordan isn't a troublemaker – he's an angel.'

In a short time, the pumpkin-bread batter was done. It was perfect. All that was left to be added were the chocolate chips.

Once again, Jordan darted in front of DB. 'Here you go, Oz, old pal,' he said, passing Oz a small bowl.

'Ah, the crowning touch,' noted the observing judge. His pen hovered over his clipboard.

Oz smiled at him. This was going better than he'd expected. Maybe Jordan and Tank weren't planning to sabotage him after all. He was just about to dump the contents of the bowl into the batter when DB grabbed his arm. Flashing a broad grin at the judge and the camera, she uttered a single word through clenched teeth: 'Don't.'

133

Oz frowned. DB covered her mouth and pretended to cough. 'It's a trap,' she said into her microphone.

Oz looked down. He gasped. Sure enough, instead of chocolate chips, the bowl contained two carefully measured cups of gravel. He looked up again. Tank and Jordan were beaming. They gave him an enthusiastic thumbs up. Just below the surface of the work table, out of the judge's sight, Jordan held up the bag of chocolate chips. He wagged it tantalizingly, then whipped it behind his back.

'Well, young man?' said the judge, glancing at his watch. 'Time's a-wasting.'

'Um,' said Oz, weighing his options. If he complained, the judge would take away their extra points for exemplary teamwork. On the other hand, if he baked the pumpkin bread with gravel in it, they'd come in last for sure. Not to mention possibly be arrested – the judges would break their teeth on the small stones.

DB turned away again and coughed into her hand. 'Code Red,' she muttered. 'Stones substituted for chocolate chips.'

'We're on it!' cried Lip from under the table. 'Stall for time.'

So far, the Acorns hadn't proved to be much use.

134

Still nestled in DB's hair, they'd ridden back from Grand Central Station to the hotel in nearly complete radio silence. Only the occasional peep or squeak as one or the other of them spotted something thrilling through the bus window had let Oz and DB know they were still there. Once in the ballroom again, they had scampered quickly down DB's back and disappeared under the long cloth that skirted the work table. Oz had almost forgotten that they were there.

Stall for time? thought Oz, his mind suddenly a blank. The camera zoomed in, and his face loomed large on the TV screen above. *What should I do?* He glanced desperately at DB, who shrugged. Spotting his mother in the crowd, Oz had a brainstorm. *The name is Levinson, Oz Levinson*, he thought, then cleared his throat and began to address the camera. 'I'd just like to say . . .' he began. He stopped. The crowd looked up at him expectantly.

'I'd just like to say that if it weren't for my mother I wouldn't be here at all,' Oz blurted.

The judge and the gathered crowd looked surprised by this sudden outburst, and Oz chuckled nervously. 'Well, that's obvious I suppose, but that's not what I meant.' This brought a tiny ripple of laughter. *Lame,* thought Oz. *Really lame.* He'd have to do better than that. 'What I mean is, this recipe is special. My mother loves pumpkin bread, and every year at Thanksgiving I make her a batch. My father taught me how.'

'Lower the bowl, Oz,' said Romeo over the headset.

As he continued to talk, Oz slowly lowered the bowl full of gravel until it was just below the edge of the work table, out of sight of the judge and the camera. At the same time, DB stepped forward, shielding him from Jordan and Tank's view. Out of the corner of his eye, Oz saw Lip, Romeo and Nutmeg scoot up the tablecloth. He tipped the bowl slightly and they dived in. There was a flurry of activity as their paws flew, pushing the gravel out. When the bowl was empty, they gave him a paws up, then scampered back down the cloth.

'Where are the chocolate chips?' asked Lip.

'The chocolate chips!' boomed Oz, startling the judge, who dropped his pen. He continued in a more normal tone. 'Um, I'm sure you're all wondering how I came up with that idea. The chocolate chips are, um, my *secret* ingredient, and I kept them *hidden* from my parents. Popped them into the batter *behind their backs*, if you get my drift.'

'OK, got your drift,' said Romeo's voice in his ear. 'We're on it.'

As Oz droned on with his speech – how much his mother loved the bread, what a nice family Thanksgiving tradition it had become – the Acorns disappeared under the tablecloth again. They reappeared a split second later at Jordan Scott's feet. Leaving his fellow band members positioned by the sixth grader's large trainer, Lip climbed silently up Jordan's trouser leg. The mouse circled around behind to where he was holding the bag of chocolate chips, then bit down on Jordan's wrist. Hard.

'Yow!' cried Jordan, releasing the bag.

Lip leaped nimbly aboard the bag as it plummeted towards the floor. The second the bag landed, he grabbed a corner, as did Romeo and Nutmeg. Before Jordan could even turn around, the mice had whisked the bag out of sight beneath the tablecloth.

Jordan stared at the floor behind him, puzzled. Next he stared at his wrist.

'What's the matter?' asked the judge.

'Lunch box,' said Oz softly, just loud enough so Jordan could hear.

'Hamster,' added DB.

Jordan's face flushed bright red. The camera

137

zoomed in. The sixth grader smiled half-heartedly. 'Uh, nothing,' he said weakly.

'And in conclusion,' said Oz, reaching down and grabbing the bag of chocolate chips that suddenly poked out from underneath the tablecloth by his feet, 'I'd just like to say that chocolate chips and Mayflower Flour are a winning combination!' He held the bag up triumphantly. Jordan and Tank gaped at him.

'How'd he do that?' muttered Tank.

Oz tore open the bag, poured the chocolate chips into the batter, and stirred it vigorously before handing the bowl to DB. She poured the batter into the pan and popped it into the oven.

'Well done,' said the judge, nodding approvingly. 'Extra points for thanking your parents.'

'Good job, Acorns,' whispered Oz.

Jordan and Tank glared.

'Dogbones and Fatboy think they're smart,' said Tank.

Jordan's eyes narrowed. 'Something weird is going on here,' he said, inspecting the tiny bite mark on his wrist. 'Something very weird. I don't know what it is yet, but we're gonna find out.'

CHAPTER EIGHTEEN

DAY TWO – WEDNESDAY 1400 HOURS

Bananas Foster poked his head into the practice room.

'Everything ready for tonight, Cherry?' he asked, his toothy smile sparkling as brightly as his diamond-studded 'B' around his neck.

'Sure,' said Glory with a confidence she didn't feel. Tonight was going to be a disaster. There was no getting around that fact. But tonight wasn't here yet, and right now Glory had more important things to think about than her ill-fated singing debut. Like getting rid of Bananas Foster.

'I'd love to talk, Bananas, but we're kind of busy

right now,' she said, batting her eyelashes at him. 'Practising, you know.'

The nightclub owner looked over at Hotspur, Bubble and Squeak. 'Your fans found you already, I see.'

'Just trying to get autographs,' said Hotspur, whipping out a piece of paper and a pen. '"The memorials and the things of fame", as the Bard says.'

'Says who?' asked Bananas, with a blank look. Before Hotspur could reply, the nightclub owner's gaze fell on the mobile phone that stood propped up against the purple dinosaur lunch box. 'What's that?'

There was a long pause, then B-Nut said, 'It's one of our props. For a new song we thought we'd try out tonight.'

'Really?' Bananas Foster's ears perked up at this. 'A new tune? What's it called?'

'Uh,' said B-Nut. 'It's called . . . it's called –'

'It's called, "Call Me, Sugarpaws",' offered Glory. 'Fabulous song, just fabulous. It'll hit number one in the charts for sure. My brother's vocals are awesome. Wait until you hear him!'

B-Nut cringed. Bananas Foster's eyes lit up with

140

delight. 'Sounds fabulous! I'll go add it to the posters right now. And I'll alert the media, too. With any luck, I can make the deadline at the *Tattletail*. We might even make page one!' He bustled out of the room.

'"Call Me, Sugarpaws"?' cried B-Nut as the door closed behind the nightclub owner. 'What am I supposed to do with *that*?'

Glory gave him a mischievous smile. 'Best I could do under pressure. Let's just say, maybe now we're even for "Cherry Jubilee".'

B-Nut shook his head unhappily. 'Well, we'd better get rolling here. Apparently I've got a song to write.'

The mice gathered around the mobile phone. Bunsen reached out and pressed a series of numbers with his paw. The tiny screen flashed to life, then went dark again.

'I thought you said this would work,' snapped Hotspur. 'Did we risk our lives for nothing?'

'I haven't finished yet,' Bunsen replied stiffly. He punched in a few more numbers, and the screen flickered to life again as the mobile phone picked up the video feed from the sewer. Bubble and Squeak drew back in alarm as Roquefort

Dupont's hideous face swam into view. There was a long gash over the rat's left eye and several of his whiskers had been yanked out.

'Looks like someone took a bite out of him,' said B-Nut.

'Stilton Piccadilly, most likely,' said Bubble. 'They were bickering all morning.'

The mobile-phone speaker crackled as the audio relay kicked in.

'GRR!' screeched Dupont.

Glory shot her colleague an admiring glance. 'Bunsen, you're a genius!'

Bunsen's nose flushed pink with pleasure at the compliment. 'It's nothing, really,' he said modestly. 'Just a bit of tinkering, that's all.'

'We call that "Bunsenizing",' Glory whispered to Bubble and Squeak, who nodded sagely. They had lab mice in London, too.

'This new wireless technology is really quite amazing,' continued Bunsen enthusiastically. 'The relays were the most difficult part. They –'

'Enough of the lab chatter,' said Hotspur rudely. 'You test-tube tails are all alike – you think we're all interested in the boring details. I for one would rather listen to the rats.'

Stung, Bunsen turned his back on Hotspur and made a great show of busying himself with the volume controls.

'And now,' announced a silky voice from the mobile-phone speaker, 'eet eez my very great *plaisir* to introduce ze Global Rodent Roundtable's keynote speaker, ze rat who has called us all together for zis momentous occasion, *mon cousin*, Roquefort Dupont!'

'Who the heck is that?' asked B-Nut, peering curiously at the screen. 'She's pretty good-looking, for a rat.'

'Brie de Sorbonne,' replied Bubble. 'And never judge a book, or a rat, by its cover. Brie positively terrorizes the guilds in Paris. She keeps our colleagues at Intertail's whiskers in a constant twist.'

'My fellow rodents, we are here today for a purpose!' thundered Dupont, his ugly face flashing on to the mobile-phone screen again. 'We are here today for a reason! We are here today because of something I see happening in my city, and something I know is happening in yours.' He paused dramatically, before leaning forward towards his audience and intoned, *'We are here because we are being outwitted by the mice at every turn!'*

'Speak for yourself,' muttered Stilton Piccadilly.

143

Dupont shot his rival a murderous glance. 'If we don't unite now and do something about it,' he continued, 'we'll keep losing ground. Soon, we'll be overrun by those wretched small-paws, and the future for rats will be bleak indeed. I say it's time for a new world order! I say it's time for this planet to finally become . . . MICE-FREE!'

Limburger Lulu and Limburger Louie appeared on the screen. 'MICE-FREE FROM SEA TO SEA! MICE-FREE FOR YOU AND ME!' they squeaked, hooking tails and dancing in a circle.

Backstage at *BANANAS!*, the mice watched, transfixed, as the leader of Washington's rodent underworld warmed to his message. Dupont began to pace back and forth in front of his foreign compatriots, his tail thrashing side to side.

'What we need is a plan. And a plan is exactly what I have to offer you today.'

'Offer us?' snarled Piccadilly suspiciously. 'And what exactly do you want in exchange for this plan of yours?'

'Me?' said Dupont innocently. 'Why, whatever made you think I'd want anything in exchange?'

Piccadilly snorted. 'Let's just say, your reputation precedes you, Dupont, you greedy, conniving –'

'Look who's talking!' Dupont's beady red eyes flashed in anger, and the two big rats started to square off again.

Once again, Brie stepped forward. 'Boys, boys,' she said, cuffing her cousin affectionately and placing a restraining paw on Stilton Piccadilly's brawny shoulder. 'We'll never get anywhere eef zees continues.'

Reluctantly, Stilton backed away. Dupont collected himself, then continued. 'As I said, I have a plan. What we rats need to do in order to squash our enemies once and for all – what we need to ensure a mice-free world –' he paused dramatically – 'is to learn to READ!'

Dupont surveyed the sewer in triumph. If he'd been expecting applause, however, it was conspicuously absent. His fellow rats were silent. They stared at him blankly.

Stilton Piccadilly burst out laughing. 'Read?' he said with an incredulous sneer. 'That's your plan? We learn to *read*?'

'No rat worth his whiskers needs books,' muttered Gorgonzola. 'Books are for humans.'

'And those miserable short-tails,' added Muenster.

Even Mozzarella Canal looked bewildered at his nephew's pronouncement. 'I don't get it, Roquefort.

Where's the fun in learning to read? Sorry, pal, but I thought you were going to declare war! You know, paw to paw, fighting it out in the streets, a nice juicy game of rat-and-mouse. That sort of thing.'

A low buzz went up as the rats began discussing Dupont's plan.

Dupont looked around the sewer desperately. 'Don't you understand?' he cried. 'Reading is the key to *everything*! Reading is what has allowed the mice to keep us down here, in the dark, a race of sewer crawlers, instead of taking our rightful place as leaders of the world! Think of it, my friends! I'm the descendant of royalty! We're all the descendants of royalty. My ancestors lived in a castle, just like yours! How many of you live in castles today?'

The rats fell silent again, considering his point.

Dupont pressed on. 'Don't you see? If we can read, we can steal mice mail, intercept mice messages, learn all the mice secrets. We'll know what makes them tick, and we'll be one jump ahead of them every step of the way. Wherever they turn, we'll be there. Whatever move they try, we'll be there. We'll outmanoeuvre, outwit and outsmart them every step of the way. All because we can READ!'

He pumped his paws in the air. 'Reading rats will

rule the WORLD!' he cried. 'Reading rats are the rats of the FUTURE! We'll make mousemeat of those small-paws! They'll be EXTERMINATED once and for ALL! Bye-bye! *Ciao! Auf Wiedersehen!* And our planet will finally be MICE-FREE!' His speech ended in a triumphant screech.

The assembled rodents burst into applause, and Dupont's rats-in-waiting scampered to the front.

'MICE-FREE FROM SEA TO SEA!' cried Limburger Lulu and Limburger Louie, as the other rats joined in the chant. 'MICE-FREE FOR YOU AND ME!'

Stilton Piccadilly swaggered forward. 'You're all talk, Dupont,' he said flatly. 'Show us a rat – any rat – who can read, and I'll show you a circus sideshow freak.'

Dupont bared his fangs at Piccadilly in a cold smile. 'I'm one step ahead of you, old chap,' he replied. He cracked his tail and Gnaw shot forward out of the shadows. 'Get me a copy of the *Tattletail*,' he ordered. 'Final street edition.'

'Yes, Boss,' said his aide, and scrabbled away.

He returned a short time later, dragging a newspaper behind him. 'Hot off the press,' he huffed, breathless from his task.

Dupont grabbed the newspaper and held it up in

his scruffy paws. 'Exhibit number one,' he announced to the Global Rodent Roundtable. 'The *Tattletail*.' He cracked his tail again. 'Scurvy, you go first.'

The bony rat scuffled reluctantly to the front of the crowd, his whiskers trailing on the floor in fear. He peered at the paper, cleared his throat, and haltingly started to read aloud. 'CALL HER SUGARPEAS!' he began.

'That's PAWS, you idiot! SugarPAWS!' snarled Dupont.

Scurvy quailed. He squinted at the newsprint doubtfully, then continued, 'ONE NIGHT ONLY! MISS CHERRY JUBILEE, STEALING ACORNS?'

'*Stealing acorns?*' said Stilton Piccadilly, shaking his head in disgust. 'This is supposed to be a useful skill? The one that will secure our future?' He eyed the crowd of rats, who stirred uneasily and muttered in disapproval. 'I'll take claws and jaws any day.'

'Give me that, you useless rodent,' Dupont snapped, grabbing the paper away from Scurvy. He scanned the headline. 'It's STEEL ACORNS, not STEALING ACORNS!' he exploded. 'Idiot.' He glared out at his compatriots. 'Steel Acorns. You know. That ridiculous mice rock band.' He looked down at the paper again, and his gaze fell on a photograph in the centre of the page. His fiery red eyes narrowed. 'Now that's a familiar set of ears,' he said softly to himself.

'THIS is your secret plan?' sneered Piccadilly. 'THIS is supposed to save our world? A concert announcement? Like I said before, you aren't fit to lead us, Dupont.'

Dupont thrust the paper into his British rival's hideous face. 'Oh yeah?' he growled. 'Take a good look at this picture. Recognize anybody? Like maybe the mouse who stole your playthings upstairs this morning?'

Stilton's face grew red with rage. 'You said her name was Glory Goldenleaf, not Cherry Jubilee!'

'She's a *spy*, you fool! She works for the Spy Mice Agency. Don't you ever go to the movies? Obviously she's here undercover. Tracking *us*. Only now – BECAUSE I CAN READ! – we've got the goods on her. And we're going to use that information – which we have why? BECAUSE I CAN READ – to take her down!'

An excited murmur arose from the other rats as the full import of Dupont's plan finally dawned on them. Dupont began to strut up and down. This new development was better than he could have imagined. Everything was going according to plan. Better than plan. He had the Global Rodent Roundtable all eating out of his paw.

'Ladies and not-so-gentle-rodents, I think this calls for a demonstration of our new strength,' he announced. 'I think this calls for –' he paused for a moment – 'a RAID!'

CHAPTER
NINETEEN

DAY TWO – WEDNESDAY 1430 HOURS

The practice room at *BANANAS!* fell dead silent as the eavesdropping mice stared at the mobile-phone screen, then at each other. A raid? Here? Tonight?

It was one thing to hear Julius calmly describe the frightening prospect of a world with literate rats, and another thing altogether to hear Dupont himself outline his plans. A future with reading rats was a truly shocking prospect, and a feeling of helplessness and doom settled over them like a cold fog.

'Mousemeat,' whispered Glory. 'We're all mousemeat. This is worse than the Black Paw.'

'Black Paw?' asked Squeak.

'Dupont's hit list,' Glory explained. 'I've been on it for a while now. He almost got me last month.'

Get a grip, Goldenleaf, she ordered herself sternly. She was beginning to make herself depressed and, as mission leader, she needed to rally the troops, not to be a fearmonger.

'Dupont may be able to read, but he doesn't have access to human technology yet,' she said briskly. 'Thanks to Bunsen, we're still one step ahead of him.'

Bunsen's nose glowed pink again.

'Plus, the rats may think they have the element of surprise, but that still belongs to us,' Glory continued. 'And we're going to use it to our advantage. They want to raid us, let them raid us. We'll be ready for them when they get here. And what's more, I think this is a golden opportunity to turn the tables on them.'

'How?' asked Squeak.

'Bait 'em,' said Glory simply. 'Plant a little misinformation. They think they can read? Fine. We'll give them something to read. Lead them right into a trap of our own. And once we've got them cornered – bam! End of rats.'

'What do we use for bait?' queried Bubble.

Glory looked around the room. 'One of us,' she replied. 'Someone who's a good actor and who won't buckle under the pressure.'

Hotspur preened. 'That would be me. As my uncle always says, "right tool for the right job",' he said, quoting Julius instead of Shakespeare for once. 'We Folgers are known for our cool heads – and for our acting skills. Living so close to the Bard as we do.'

Glory had to admit this was true. Some of the Entertainment Guild's brightest stars had grown up at the Shakespeare Folger Library. Hotspur's own sister, Ophelia, for one. She narrowed her eyes, considering. Glory was pretty sure that Snotspur smelt the spotlight of fame. A major coup against the rats – and not just one rat, but a whole pack of international kingpin rats – would be a career boost beyond his wildest dreams. Glory could practically see him measuring her tail, to see how much of it he could step on in his rush up the Spy Mice Agency ladder. Well, this was her show, her mission, her first big break and she wasn't about to let him snatch it away from her. Or steal the credit.

'No, Hotspur,' she said. 'You heard him – it's me that Dupont wants. And it's me he's going to get.'

Bunsen gave a squeak of alarm. 'What!' he protested. 'Glory, we can't send you into the lion's den – er, rat's lair. Not again.'

'The lab mouse is right, for once,' agreed Hotspur.

He flexed his bicep. 'This is a job for a stronger, more seasoned Silver Skateboard agent.'

'Nobody's sending me anywhere, Bunsen,' Glory said, ignoring Hotspur. 'I'm volunteering. "The noblest motive is the public good", remember?'

'The Spy Mice Agency motto,' Bunsen replied glumly.

'I'm not sure this is such a good idea,' cautioned B-Nut. 'You barely got out alive last time you pulled this kind of a stunt. I think we should run it by Julius first.'

Glory nodded. 'Fair enough,' she said. 'We'll email him as soon as we hammer out a plan. And once we get a paws up, we'll send a pigeon post to Oz and DB. Gather round, spy mice. Here's what we're going to do.'

CHAPTER
TWENTY

DAY TWO – WEDNESDAY 1545 HOURS

Lavinia Levinson gazed down at the sheet of paper in her hand. 'This is for a school project?' she asked.

'Uh-huh,' said Oz, squirming slightly at the fib. He consoled himself that it was for a worthy cause. Plus, it was true that every experience he'd had with the mice was educational. He was learning to become a secret agent, wasn't he?

Mrs Levinson tapped out the lively beat on the coffee table in front of her and hummed a few bars. 'It's good,' she said in surprise. 'Catchy tune. And I love the title, "Born to Shake My Tail". Did you two write this?'

Oz and DB exchanged a glance.

'No, a friend of ours wrote it,' Oz replied.

His mother raised an eyebrow. 'A fifth grader?'

'Um, no – he's a little older. Teenager. We met him at the Spy Museum.' Oz thrust the microcassette recorder into his mother's hand. 'Just sing into the microphone, OK? And don't sing it like your normal stuff. Not that your normal stuff is bad!' he hastened to add. 'It's just this is more, you know, rock music.'

DB glanced at her watch. 'We should hurry,' she said. 'They're going to announce the bake-off winners soon downstairs.'

'Pushy, pushy,' said Lavinia Levinson in mock complaint. 'You're worse than one of my conductors.' She rose from the hotel-room sofa, took a deep breath, and began to sing.

TWENTY-ONE

DAY TWO – WEDNESDAY 1700 HOURS

Roquefort Dupont stared up at the giant TV screen on the wall of the dining concourse at Grand Central Station.

The Global Rodent Roundtable had broken up for dinner. The rats had agreed that filling their bellies in preparation for the raid was the first order of business. Dupont's Uncle Mozzarella was leading one group on a tour of the skips of Little Italy, world-famous for their delicious pasta and cannoli pastries and other Italian delicacies. Gorgonzola, for whom that wasn't anything special, was escorting Brie and

another contingent to Chinatown instead. Limburger Lulu and Limburger Louie had gone with them, practically sick with excitement at the prospect of an outing.

Dupont had remained behind at Grand Central Station with Scurvy and Gnaw. He was in the mood for shellfish, and the Oyster Bar was one of the best spots in town to indulge. Plus, he wanted to practise his speech for later tonight. He had the nomination in the bag, he was sure of it.

'The twenty-fifth annual Mayflower Flour Bake-off results are in!' blared the television. Dupont slurped an oyster and watched idly as footage from the Waldorf-Astoria's ballroom rolled. 'This year's winner, in the Adult Division, is Mrs Mary Lou Swenson of Oshkosh, Wisconsin, for her cheese twists,' announced the enthusiastic reporter. 'In the Junior Division, the top prize went to Ozymandias Levinson and Delilah Bean, students at Chester B. Arthur Elementary School in Washington DC, for their delicious pumpkin chocolate-chip bread.' The reporter popped a piece in her mouth. 'Mmmm, mmmmm. Delicious. Good job, kids.'

The camera zoomed in on Oz and DB, who held

up a plate displaying their blue-ribbon-adorned results.

'I've seen those humans some place before,' muttered Dupont. He whirled around. 'Scurvy! Gnaw!'

His two aides, who had been scuffling over the remains of a cheeseburger, looked up. Scurvy's snout was covered in ketchup.

'Look at the TV!' ordered Dupont. 'Do those kids look familiar to you?'

Scurvy shrugged his narrow shoulders. Gnaw sucked the cheese off his whiskers and peered closer.

'I'm very happy to have won,' said Oz, prodding nervously at his glasses. 'It's quite an honour.' Beside him, DB nodded politely.

'I swear I recognize those voices,' mused Dupont.

'Aren't those the two we chased at Hallowe'en?' asked Gnaw. 'The ones who caught you in the net?'

Dupont stiffened. 'I thought I told you never to mention the H-word again.'

Gnaw's lone ear trembled as Dupont advanced menacingly towards him. 'But, Boss, it's them! You wanted to know,' he whined, cowering.

Dupont glared at him, then whirled around and stared at the TV once again.

'So there you have it, folks,' concluded the reporter. 'The lucky winners! Stay tuned for our coverage tomorrow morning, when they'll be featured on Mayflower Flour's fabulous float in our fabulous city's fabulous Macy's Thanksgiving Day parade!'

'Fabulous,' growled Dupont. 'Just fabulous.' A speculative glint appeared in his repulsive red eyes, and he waddled over to his aides. 'Whaddya say, boys? I think tomorrow's forecast calls for cloudy with a chance of rats, don't you?'

Scurvy and Gnaw gaped at their boss. He smiled slyly.

'Yes, indeed,' continued Dupont, 'that's one parade that's gonna get rained on for sure.' He leaned towards his aides, who shrank back from his rancid breath. 'It's payback time,' he whispered.

CHAPTER
TWENTY-TWO

DAY TWO – WEDNESDAY 2130 HOURS

High above Rockefeller Plaza, underneath the famous Rainbow Room, the dance floor of *BANANAS!* was rocking and rolling.

'Call me, Sugarpaws, call me!' B-Nut sang. Behind him, Lip and Romeo kept up a loud electric wail, while Nutmeg forged a driving beat on the drums.

Glory, anxiously awaiting her turn, watched from the stage wings. The female mice, as usual, were swooning over her handsome rocker-pilot brother. Judging by their response, 'Call Me, Sugarpaws', composed just a few short hours ago, was most definitely a hit. It was also the lead-in to the Acorns' number-one tune, 'Born to Shake My Tail' – and her debut as Cherry Jubilee.

'Good luck out there tonight, Cherry.'

Glory swung around. Like the Cheshire cat, all that was visible of Bananas Foster in the darkness backstage was his smile. That and the diamond 'B' slung around his neck.

'Thanks, Bananas,' Glory replied, trying not to sound nervous.

'No, my dear Cherry, thank *you*,' replied the nightclub owner. 'You and the Acorns really packed the place.' He looked out at the dance floor and rubbed his paws together. 'Look at them! They're going bananas!' He chuckled. 'Get it? Going *bananas*?'

'I get it,' said Glory wearily. Bananas Foster was a pest.

'So, Cherry, are you busy after the show?'

You could say that, thought Glory. If you called willingly allowing yourself to be captured by the world's meanest, ugliest, scariest rat being 'busy'. Aloud, she replied, 'Uh, yeah. Sorry.'

Disappointed, the nightclub owner bent over her paw and gave it a long smooch. Glory resisted the urge to pull it away. *You are Cherry Jubilee, rock star,* she told herself sternly. *You are used to having male fans make fools of themselves over you.*

'Until we meet again, then,' said Bananas, his smile

gleaming in the darkness once more.

'I'll be counting the minutes,' Glory purred in her best mouse-fatale voice. No point arousing his suspicions this late in the game.

As B-Nut swung into the final refrain ('Whether it's night or whether it's day, if you gotta work or if you wanna play, just call me, Sugarpaws, call me!'), Bunsen materialized, his white coat shining like a full moon in the backstage gloom.

'Are you sure this is going to work?' Glory said anxiously, as her colleague adjusted the beaded collar that encircled her elegant neck.

'Trust me, it will work,' Bunsen replied, tugging at a decorative cluster of cherries – made from red sequins foraged from a sweater left in the Rainbow Room's lost and found – to make sure they were secure. 'The microphone is hidden inside the centre cherry. Just give me the signal when you're ready to sing.'

Glory looked out at the crowd again. No doubt about it, she had a full-blown case of stage fright. As if she didn't have enough on her paws already, what with the looming prospect of another run-in with Roquefort Dupont. She took a few deep breaths and tried to quell her rising panic.

'The note is taped to the inside of your collar,'

Bunsen continued. 'Dupont can't miss it. It's not in code, and I wrote the words in really big letters. Even he'll be able to read them.'

Glory's plan had been given an enormous boost by Oz and DB winning the bake-off. In fact, that had been the clincher for Julius, who had been reluctant at first to agree. 'Too dangerous,' he'd said. 'I don't want to risk my best agents.' Once Oz sent news via pigeon post of his victory, however, Glory had emailed Julius again, and this time he'd said yes.

'You're right, the parade is a once-in-a-lifetime opportunity,' the Spy Mice Agency director had written back, giving the mission his seal of approval. 'But be careful.'

Her plan was completely foolproof, Glory was sure of it. She reviewed it mentally one more time, just to make sure she hadn't overlooked any loopholes. Any time now, Dupont would raid the nightclub and take her captive. He'd find the note under her collar with the false information – information that would lead him to believe the mice were planning to rendezvous with Oz and DB aboard the Mayflower Flour float at the end of tomorrow's parade. Confronting the mice there for a showdown would be irresistible to Dupont. The float's balloon *Mayflower*

was nearly as big as his ego, after all. When he showed up in Herald Square, however, the mice would already be aboard with Oz and DB, waiting for him. They'd have the upper paw, and victory was inevitable. Yes, it was the perfect rat-trap. Nothing could go wrong. *Then why am I so afraid?* Glory wondered.

'Bunsen, I'm scared!' she blurted, clutching her colleague's paw.

'Of what?'

'Dupont,' said Glory. 'And the rest of the rats.' She swallowed hard, trying to keep her voice from shaking. 'I keep remembering the looks on Bubble and Squeak's faces when they were tied to Stilton Piccadilly's tail, and thought they were going to die. It's the same way I felt when I was trapped in Dupont's lair, before you and B-Nut came to rescue me.'

'I told you this was a completely insane idea!' Bunsen cried. He patted her paw anxiously. 'Don't worry, it's not too late to call it off. I've got a smoke bomb in the lunch box backstage – we'll fake a fire. Clear out the club in nothing flat. We'll all be gone before the rats even get here.'

Glory shook her head. 'No. We can't back out now.'

'Then send Hotspur instead.' Bunsen brightened at this prospect.

165

Glory stiffened. 'I am *not* sending Hotspur,' she said stubbornly. 'He doesn't know Dupont like I do.'

'Are you sure that isn't just the famous Goldenleaf pride talking?' said Bunsen, a bit sharply. 'If you don't want to send Hotspur, you could send me or B-Nut. We've both had first-paw experience with Dupont before, too.'

Glory dropped her gaze. 'It's not just pride, Bunsen,' she protested, though if she really admitted the truth to herself, there was a bit of that involved. This was her first Silver Skateboard mission, after all, her chance to prove herself to Julius and the agency. Glory had no intention of letting Hotspur steal the credit – which he would gladly do, given half a chance, she was sure of it. Hotspur was poised to pounce at the first sign of weakness from her, she could tell. Glory squared her shoulders. 'I'll be fine.'

Bunsen didn't look convinced. 'I still think this is a bad idea,' he told her.

His words were nearly drowned out in the roar of applause from the nightclub as the Steel Acorns finished their new tune. Bananas Foster sprang up on to the stage and took the microphone. 'You heard it here first, mouselings!' he announced. 'Another Steel Acorns hit in the making! And now, I have the pleasure of introducing a rising star. Here in the Big Apple for one night only, the very talented, the very lovely Miss Cherry Jubilee!'

Bunsen poked Glory in the back. 'You're on,' he whispered. 'Knock 'em dead. Bananas is right, by the way. You look beautiful.'

Glory smiled at him. 'Thanks, Bunsen. You're true blue.' Blinking in the bright spotlights, she shuffled reluctantly onstage and peered out at the dance floor. Hotspur and Squeak were there posing as a couple, while Bubble unobtrusively patrolled the crowd with a squad of elite Mouse Guards. Undercover back-up had been Julius's sole condition for the mission. 'We can't risk civilian casualties,' he had said.

Stiffen your whiskers, Glory told herself sharply, pushing thoughts of the coming raid out of her mind. *Focus on the job in hand.*

Bunsen gave her an enthusiastic paws-up from the wings as the crowd started to applaud in anticipation. Nutmeg launched into the energetic percussion lead-in, and Glory began tapping her tail to the beat. As the familiar rhythm flowed through her, Glory relaxed slightly. She took a deep breath and looked over to where Bunsen was waiting. She nodded. The lab mouse signalled the Acorns, and Lip and Romeo

167

struck the opening chords of 'Born to Shake My Tail'. The dance floor went wild.

Here goes nothing, thought Glory, closing her eyes and opening her mouth. She hoped fervently that whatever came out wouldn't spell disaster for the mission. A bullfrog with laryngitis would definitely blow their cover.

'BORN TO DANCE, BORN TO WAIL,' sang a voice. A gorgeous soprano voice. Glory's eyes flew open. She almost forgot to keep mouthing the words. 'BORN TO SHAKE MY TAIL!' sang Oz's mother, as Glory lip-synched the lyrics. The explosive guitar riffs and driving beat brought every mouse in the club to his or her hindpaws, and in a whisker the whole place was rocking along to the hit song.

Onstage, Glory, too, began to wiggle to the beat as she continued to lip-sync the words. 'I'm a hard-rockin' mouse, and I bring down the house, every time I twitch my tail!' Out on the dance floor, Hotspur and Squeak Savoy started a conga line. Squeak waved at her, and Glory waved back. 'I feel the beat with my paws, and hit the dance floor because – the music starts me groovin' without fail!'

The song continued to flow without a hitch. Glory was totally into her role by the time she reached the refrain: 'BORN TO DANCE, BORN TO WAIL, BORN TO SHAKE MY TAIL!' As she finished, the crowd erupted in cheers.

'Cher-ry! Cher-ry! Cher-ry!' they chanted, begging for more. Glory looked over at Bunsen, aghast. They hadn't rehearsed an encore! Oz's mother hadn't recorded an encore! What was she supposed to do?

She never got a chance to find out.

The doors to the nightclub burst open and Roquefort Dupont charged in. Stilton Piccadilly, Muenster the Monster and Mozzarella Canal were right behind him.

'RATS!' someone screamed. 'IT'S A RAID!'

In a whisker, all was pandemonium. The packed dance floor emptied as the panicked mice scattered, pushing and shoving each other in a frantic attempt to flee the advancing rats. Bubble and the Mouse Guards herded as many of the nightclub's patrons as they could to safety backstage, and Glory saw Bananas Foster scramble for cover, too. Her last glimpse of him was a flash from the diamond 'B' around his neck as he dived behind one of the giant plastic bananas that flanked the stage.

'There she is!' screamed Dupont, spotting her. 'She's the one I want!'

It's show time, thought Glory. She scampered across the stage and pretended to trip on the microphone cord.

'Good luck, Sis,' called B-Nut as he ran past, followed by the Acorns. Hotspur and Squeak were right behind them.

For one wild moment, Glory wondered whether Bunsen was right, that this was a completely insane idea. She could see the lab mouse out of the corner of her eye, his white fur gleaming in the spotlights as he hesitated by the stage curtain.

'GO!' she shouted, waving him frantically away. The mission couldn't risk Bunsen falling into rat paws. His technological expertise was the heart and soul of their operation. Glory saw her colleague turn reluctantly to leave, and she breathed a sigh of relief.

It was short-lived. Dupont leaped onstage and advanced towards her with a malevolent grin. Glory got to her hindpaws and backed away, eyes wide in what was supposed to be mock fear. Only there was nothing 'mock' about what she was feeling. She'd forgotten how big Dupont was. And how ugly and fierce and evil. His red eyes glowed like fiery embers and, when he opened his mouth to speak, the stench of his breath nearly curled her whiskers.

'Well, if it isn't little Glory Goldenleaf!' said Roquefort Dupont. 'Or should I say Cherry Jubilee?'

He lunged at her, and Glory dived towards the stage wings, all pretence gone. The only thing she could think of now was getting away from Dupont and the other rats crowding on to the stage behind him.

Her paws scrabbled frantically on the stage's smooth wooden surface. Dupont caught her by the tail and reeled her in like a fish. Glory struggled mightily, but it was useless. In a trice, he had her in his powerful grip. He grabbed her by the scruff of her neck and shook her violently. The red sequin cherries popped off her collar one by one and rolled into the shadows.

'Looks like it's bye-bye, Cherry Jubilee, and hello, Glory Goldenleaf,' snarled Dupont. He bared his fangs in a triumphant smile. 'You're coming with us.'

CHAPTER
TWENTY-THREE

DAY TWO –
WEDNESDAY
2200 HOURS

Bound, blindfolded, gagged and slung over Dupont's shoulder by her tail, Glory jolted up and down, her teeth rattling like dice in a cup.

'Through here!' Dupont ordered. 'Quick!'

Glory heard the sharp rasp of claws on metal as the rats hustled her into the building's ventilation shaft. 'See you at the bottom, boys!' Dupont called, and Glory felt her stomach drop as her captor dived head first into the web of ducts that snaked down through 30 Rockefeller Plaza. Slipping and sliding they plunged, down, down, down, bumping and crashing as they went. Rat transport was much rougher than riding a skateboard. As she was flung from side to side, her little head banging against the hard metal at every turn, Glory wished fervently that she had her safety helmet.

'This way!' Dupont cried, his voice echoing on the hard cement floor as they finally emerged into the cavernous basement. Again Glory heard the click of claws, and again her stomach dropped as they plunged downward. Only this time they weren't travelling through a ventilation shaft – this time, they were travelling through the sewer. Glory's nose told her so. She wrinkled it in distaste, recalling the stench only too well from her last run-in with Dupont in his lair back in Washington.

They splashed on through the slimy subterranean tunnels and the rats fell silent, breathing hard. From somewhere far above Glory heard the screech of metal wheels against metal tracks as a subway train clattered by. They were heading, Glory was fairly sure, for Track Seventy-seven at Grand Central Station.

Finally, Dupont halted, panting. He let go of Glory's tail, and she tumbled down his back, landing with a splash in a deep puddle. Coughing and choking through her gag, she scrabbled with her hindpaws, frantically trying to keep her head above water. Dupont was trying to drown her!

Dupont gave a soft chuckle. 'It's not going to be that easy,' he said, as if reading her thoughts. 'I have other plans for you.'

Jerking her up out of the sewer water, he removed her blindfold and ripped off her gag. Glory cried out as several of her whiskers were torn off along with it.

'It's no use screaming for help,' Dupont told her. 'No one can hear you.'

'So zis is ze famous Glory you are always talking about, *mon cher*,' Glory heard a soft female voice say. She squirmed around in Dupont's grasp to find herself eye to eye with Brie de Sorbonne. 'What eez so special about zees particular mouse?' Glory detected a note of jealousy in the she-rat's voice. She flinched as Brie reached out and stroked her fur. 'Her coat eez thick and warm, *oui* – good for slippers, perhaps, or a nice winter hat. Otherwise, she eez quite ordinary in appearance.'

Slippers? A hat? Glory's heart beat faster. Was that to be her fate, then, to wind up as accessories for this Coco Chanel with fangs?

'Don't let appearances fool you,' Dupont growled in reply. 'This is no ordinary mouse.' His voice had a cold edge, and Glory felt a chill run down her spine.

The other Global Rodent Roundtable delegates crowded forward and sniffed her curiously. Their breath was as nasty as Dupont's, and Glory recoiled.

'So this is the fearless Morning Glory Goldenleaf?' sneered Stilton Piccadilly. 'Not so fearless now, are you?'

Gorgonzola, his low-slung belly skimming the wet surface of the sewer floor, crept closer. He eyed Glory, licking his lips. She shrank back in terror, heart pounding. Were the rumours true? Was Gorgonzola a mousivore? Before she could find out, Dupont thrust Glory up over his head in triumph.

'Behold the power of the written word!' he cried, his voice echoing along the dank walls of the sewer. 'I came, I read, I conquered! Now let the proceedings begin!'

Limburger Lulu and Limburger Louie crept forward. Taking their places on either side of Roquefort Dupont, they began to sing. Their high ratling voices hadn't achieved the harshness of full rodent adulthood and, while nowhere near the calibre of Lavinia Levinson, they weren't entirely unpleasant. Glory listened, curiosity momentarily overriding her fear.

'Who will it be?' they sang, as the mob of rats formed a circle, tails linked in a hairless chain.

'Who is the rat we will choose for Big Cheese?'

They're selecting a leader, Glory thought with a start. *They're going to crown a rat king!*

Brie stepped forward. 'Members of ze Global Rodent Roundtable!'

'GRR!' answered the mob.

'Ze time has come to let your voices be heard! Ze time has come to make your choice! Roquefort Dupont or Stilton Piccadilly, who will we elect as Big Cheese?'

'Some choice,' muttered Glory. 'Rat scum or rat poison.'

Brie whirled around. 'Gag her again,' she snarled, and Scurvy rushed to obey.

Roquefort Dupont and Stilton Piccadilly stepped to the centre of the ring.

'Eez there anything more you boys would like to say before ze vote?' asked Brie.

'My record speaks for itself,' boasted Piccadilly.

From their places in the surrounding circle, Gorgonzola and Muenster nodded in agreement.

Dupont cleared his throat. 'Your choice is clear – tradition versus innovation. Old school versus new school. A rat of the past, or a rat of the future. Me! Roquefort Dupont!' He thumped his chest with a filthy paw, then paused. 'I have a confession to make: I've been holding out on you.'

'This is an outrage!' cried Stilton Piccadilly. 'I protest! He's trying to steal the election!'

'Steal the election? Nonsense,' said Dupont with a dismissive wave of his paw. He glanced around slyly. 'Doesn't anybody want to see my secret weapon?'

'Now you're talking!' cried Mozzarella Canal. 'Weapons are more like it!' He turned to the big Greek rat beside him. 'See, Misery, all that talk about books was just a bluff. I knew my nephew wouldn't let us down. Claws and jaws always win in the end.'

Dupont's smile broadened. He turned and beckoned towards a side-tunnel. 'Come on out,' he said.

A small figure stepped from the shadows. Glory squinted in the gloom, trying to make out who it was. Another ratling?

'The first thing you need to do,' said the small figure quietly, so quietly that his words weren't picked up by the audio feed on the sunglasses suspended above, 'is get rid of those.' He raised his paw and pointed towards the sewer vent overhead.

Glory gasped. It was Fumble.

CHAPTER
TWENTY-FOUR

Backstage in the practice room at *BANANAS!*, the eavesdropping mice stared at the mobile-phone screen in consternation.

'Something's wrong!' cried Bunsen. 'Look! Something's wrong with Glory!'

Her paws twisted cruelly behind her back, her gag silencing her once again, Glory bounced up and down in frustration, struggling to free her-self from Dupont's firm grip.

'Mmm-mm!' she squeaked frantically. 'Mmm-mm!'

'She's trying to tell us something,' said B-Nut, staring at his sister.

'I told her this would never work!' cried Bunsen in despair. 'I – I mean we – never should have let her go!'

Onscreen, the rats suddenly tilted their heads back and stared directly at the mice. The remote camera tracked their movement, and the mobile-phone screen reflected a mass of red, glowing eyes. Seventy-seven pairs of eyes, to be exact.

'Uh-oh,' said B-Nut. 'That's not good.'

'They spotted the sunglasses,' observed Bubble. 'That must be what Glory is trying to tell us.'

The mice watched in worried fascination as Brie de Sorbonne slinked towards the sewer wall and began to scale its slick brick surface. Her face loomed across the screen for a split second, her fangs appeared, and then a jumble of images flashed across the screen as she bit through the dental floss holding the sunglasses in place and they tumbled downward to the sewer floor.

There was a splash of approaching claws as the rats ran to the windfall.

'MMM-MM! MMM-MM!' came Glory's mumbled message again, louder and more frantic than before.

'Oh, I do wish we knew what she was trying to tell us!' cried Bunsen, wringing his paws in despair.

A trio of long, ugly snouts popped on to the screen. The audio feed relayed a cacaphony of snorts and sniffs as the rats inspected the sunglasses.

'Dupont's bluffing,' they heard Stilton sneer. 'These are just ordinary human sunglasses.'

'No,' growled a deep voice.

'*Gorgonzilla!*' said Squeak with a shudder.

'Something is not right. Something is strange,' the elderly Italian rat continued.

Suddenly, Dupont's face loomed into view. He smiled, his sharp yellow fangs magnified by the videocamera. The mice drew back in alarm.

'That is one scary dude,' said Lip.

'You mice think you're clever, don't you?' Dupont said, addressing them directly. 'Well, let me tell you something – your day is over. *Finito. Ende. Ciao!* It's time for a whole new world order! It's time we rats took our rightful place as rulers! It's time for this planet to go MICE-FREE!'

In the background, above Glory's urgent mumbling, the mice could hear the other rats as they took up the chant. 'Dupont! Dupont! Dupont!'

Dupont bared his fangs again. 'Yes!' he cried in triumph. 'Yes! I am Roquefort Dupont! I am your leader! I am the BIG CHEESE!'

He opened his jaws wide. There was a loud 'SNAP!' as he severed the sunglasses in two. The mobile-phone screen blinked once and went dead.

CHAPTER
TWENTY-FIVE

'Smile for the camera!' called Amelia Bean.

'I do not believe she hasn't put that thing down by now,' whispered DB to Oz through gritted teeth. 'My cheeks hurt from smiling.'

They were sitting in a horse-drawn carriage in front of Central Park, about to take a ride to celebrate their bake-off victory. As DB's mother climbed in and sat down beside Lavinia Levinson, the driver urged his horse forward. Oz pulled the heavy blanket up to his chin. It was cold. Late, too – nearly midnight. He yawned. It had been a long day. The steady clip-clop of the horse's hooves was soothing, so was the steady drone of the two grown-ups' voices. Oz's eyelids started to droop.

'Ouch!' he cried, sitting bolt upright. DB had elbowed him in the ribs. Her elbow was bony, and it hurt. 'What'd you do that for?'

DB jerked her chin skyward. A pigeon was circling

overhead. It was Vinnie. 'Incoming,' she warned.

Oz waited until his mother and Amelia Bean turned their heads to admire the moonlight on a nearby pond, then gave Vinnie a thumbs up. The pigeon swooped down and dropped a scroll of paper into his lap. Oz whisked it under the blanket.

'Do you have a torch?' he whispered to DB, as their mothers resumed their conversation.

'Does Roquefort Dupont have a tail?' she whispered back, holding up a small penlight.

Oz slid the cipher disk from his pocket. He lifted a corner of the blanket, unrolled the pigeon post and shone the light on the tiny page. Squinting, he began mentally decoding its message.

'What does it say?' DB asked.

'"FOR YOUR PAWS ONLY,"' Oz replied.

'I know that part already. The rest of it, I mean.'

'"MISSION LAUNCHED. PROCEEDING ACCORDING TO PLAN. FULL STEAM AHEAD FOR TOMORROW."'

Oz and DB exchanged a glance. If everything was proceeding according to plan, that meant Glory was in Dupont's clutches.

'Good luck, Glory,' Oz whispered to himself. His tiny friend was going to need it.

CHAPTER
TWENTY-SIX

'Now *that* is a rat,' said Roquefort Dupont, gazing up in admiration at the towering skeleton of a Tyrannosaurus rex.

Outside, a full moon shone in the sky over Manhattan. It glinted through the high windows of the Museum of Natural History's fourth floor, bathing the bones in an eerie light. Dupont waved a paw expansively at the exhibit, as if it were his own personal possession. 'Look at that tail!' he crowed. 'Look at those sharp teeth! Definitely a rat.'

The delegates of the Global Rodent Roundtable nodded.

'*Si*,' said Gorgonzola.

'*Ja*,' agreed Muenster.

'*Oui, absolutement*,' purred Brie.

Even Stilton Piccadilly looked impressed.

Clearly relishing his new role as Big Cheese, Dupont swaggered about in front of the group, his eyes glowing red in the moonlight. 'You see what I'm telling you? This is our history! We are the descendants of giants, my friends, giants! Once we roamed the earth proudly, like old Rex here, and with me leading the Global Rodent Roundtable –'

'GRR!' growled the assembled rats automatically.

'– this will be our destiny once again. We rats will crush those small-paws like the vermin they are! Cats and dogs will tremble at our name! Even humans will call us master! Rats will be SUPREME! Rats will RULE THE WORLD!'

From where she had been unceremoniously dumped under a nearby bench, Glory gave a tiny snort. *Descendants of giants, my paw!* she thought in disgust. The only thing T-Rex-sized about Roquefort Dupont was his ego. More likely he'd sprung from some prehistoric cockroach.

She shifted uncomfortably on the hard marble floor and glared at the stout grey mouse who was guarding her. 'How could you do it, Fumble?' she asked. 'How could you be such a turn-tail?'

She still couldn't believe that a mouse – *any* mouse, even a little weasel like Fumble – would sell out to the rats. Nothing like this had ever happened before. It was completely unprecedented in mouse history.

Fumble yawned. He placed a plump paw under his chin, as if thinking the question over. 'Let's see, riches, power, fame and – dare I say it? – *glory*,' he replied calmly.

'You traitor!' spat Glory.

'Traitor to what?' countered Fumble, his voice rising in anger. 'A bunch of self-important field agents bossed around by a pathetic old has-been? Julius is so blind he can't even recognize talent when it's right under his whiskers. Well, I'll tell you right now, I won't be overlooked any more! I've had it with "silver skateboard" this and "secret mission" that. I'm fed up with stupid "For Your Paws Only"! No more being shoved aside, taken for granted, passed over!'

'So *that's* what this is all about?' sputtered Glory in disbelief. 'The fact that Julius didn't promote you to field agent?' Her bright little eyes widened as another thought occurred to her. 'It was you who taught Dupont to read, wasn't it?'

'So what if I did?' Fumble retorted. 'I'm not ashamed of it.'

'But don't you see what you've done? How could you betray us all like that?'

'How?' sneered Fumble. 'Easy, that's how. Why? Because I'm smart. Because I can tell which way the wind is blowing. Because there's a new day coming, and I intend to be part of it.'

'A new day!' Glory leaned towards her colleague. *Make that former colleague*, she corrected herself. 'Fumble, this is *Dupont*, remember? He'll chew you up and spit you out like a mouldy French fry.' *Except, of course, that a little mould never bothered Dupont*, she thought. Dupont never spat anything out.

'He's going to make me Minister of Mouse Affairs,' said Fumble smugly. 'When the Global Rodent Roundtable takes over, you and all the others will come crawling to me. Just you wait and see.'

'That's right,' Dupont interjected, waddling closer. Behind him the mob of rodents closed in. 'Once I'm in control, you mice – those we don't exterminate – will be our servants. Slaves to the master race. But I'll keep a pawful of smart ones on hand to help us learn everything we need to learn. Smart ones like Fumble here.'

He clapped Fumble on the shoulder. Fumble smirked. Glory stared at the two of them and shuddered. She recognized the look in Fumble's eyes now – it was greed. The same madness that infected Roquefort Dupont. Fumble had clearly gone round the bend. No mouse in his right mind would ever betray his own kind.

Gorgonzola lurched towards her. He lifted his snout and gave a hearty sniff. 'Smells like antipasto to me,' he said, flicking a glance at Dupont. 'Don't you agree? To celebrate your election victory, of course.' He turned back to Glory and leaned closer, so close his whiskers tickled her face. 'In Rome, we like little mouses like you,' he whispered. 'A little garlic, a little olive oil, and *presto!*' He kissed his paw in the age-old gesture of his native country. 'Dinner is served.'

Glory recoiled in horror. So the rumours about Gorgonzola were true: he *was* a mousivore! Her heart thudding like a jackhammer, she squirmed as far back underneath the bench as she could get from the massive rat and his evil appetite.

Muenster, the big black rat from Berlin, reached

188

into the shadows and plucked her out again. He smiled, and the scar along his snout puckered. '*Ja*, we like mice in Berlin, too.' He rubbed his dark belly and licked his lips. '*Maus mit Sauerkraut*, mmmm.'

Glory couldn't help it. She began to shake uncontrollably.

'Uh, comrades,' said Dupont, 'I hate to disappoint you, but I have other plans for this mouse, remember?'

Brie slinked her way over to her cousin and rested her sleek snout on his shoulder.

'But surely zis one cannot be so important?' she pouted. 'What eez one less mouse in zis world tonight?' The she-rat reached out a paw and stroked Glory's elegant brown fur. 'Such lovely things zis would make. Eet seems a shame to let it go to waste.' Brie snuggled a little closer to Dupont and scratched him behind one large flea-bitten ear. 'Give ze boys here a treat, and let me have ze rest, *oui*, Roquefort?'

Gorgonzola and Muenster looked at their new Big Cheese hopefully. Glory trembled in the German rat's tight grasp. Roquefort Dupont's Wall of Trophies and the Black Paw seemed positively tame compared to these lunatics! She didn't know which was worse, the flesh-eating mousivore twins or Cruella de Brie.

Dupont eyed the three of them, considering. He shook his head. 'No,' he said. 'She stays alive until tomorrow when we reach Times Square. After I've finished with her, you can have what's left.'

Muenster tossed Glory back under the bench, and he and Gorgonzola moved away, grumbling. Brie shrugged and slinked off, casting one more calculating look back at Glory as she went. Dupont followed her.

Glory sagged against the cold stone of the floor. Dupont might have just given her a few hours' reprieve, but he had also issued her death sentence. Tomorrow in Times Square! A tear trickled down her furry cheek. Her supposedly foolproof plan had backfired completely. *And it's all Fumble's fault,* she thought bitterly. *The traitor.* Back at Grand Central Station, once the video sunglasses had been dispensed with, it hadn't taken Fumble two seconds to reach inside her collar and pluck out the note.

'Right where your email to Julius said it would be,' he'd said smugly.

The gag had only partly muffled Glory's gasp. Fumble had intercepted their communications with Central Command! That meant Fumble knew what they were planning. And if Fumble knew, Dupont knew. She had known in that very moment she was doomed – that they were all doomed. Her friends would be walking into a trap tomorrow, and she had no way of warning them.

And worse, when this was all over, Fumble would waltz right back to the Spy Mice Agency with no one the wiser. A spy spying on the spies. A mole of the very worst sort. Not only their mission, but the whole agency – no, the entire mouse world – was in peril.

As the other rats had watched, Dupont unfolded the note. 'F-O-R Y-O-U-R P-E-A-S O-N-L-Y,' he'd read slowly aloud.

'Uh, that's *paws*, Roquefort buddy. For your paws only,' Fumble had corrected.

'I can see that, you idiot!' Dupont had snarled back, cuffing him. Dupont didn't like being corrected. He'd added huffily, 'That's what I said, anyway. "For Your Paws Only". That means top secret,' he'd informed his fellow rats, swelling with importance.

He'd stumbled through the rest of the note, which outlined Glory's fictitious rendezvous in Herald Square in front of Macy's, but Fumble had dismissed it with a flip of his paw. 'It's a trap,' he'd explained. 'They're setting you up.'

'Setting us up, are they? We'll see about that.' Dupont's eyes had narrowed. 'I think we'll just have

191

to turn the tables. Make this a parade no one will ever forget. Kids and mice together – twice the revenge for half the effort. My kind of odds.'

And now, here they all were at the Museum of Natural History, waiting for morning. It hadn't taken Dupont long at all to come up with a counterplan. First order of business: move the Global Rodent Roundtable uptown.

'Might as well stay warm while we wait,' Dupont had said, herding them all on to the underside of a B train. 'No point sitting on a parade balloon in the cold and the dark when you can be inside with a full stomach.'

As usual, food was foremost on Dupont's mind. He and the other rats had raided the museum cafe's waste bins gleefully, then dragged their smelly booty up to the fourth floor. From this vantage point, they could keep an eye on the half-inflated balloons outside and gloat over the dead bones of their supposed ancestors.

I'm going to be dead bones if I don't find a way to get out of here, thought Glory. She gazed around at the gigantic skeletons. This place was giving her the creeps.

She closed her eyes. Her small body ached from

the rough treatment she'd received, and her heart had never been heavier. *I'm going to die,* she thought miserably, and another tear trickled down her cheek. What was worse, so were Bunsen and her brother and maybe even Oz and DB, too. The children would have received their pigeon post telling them of the plan by now. Tomorrow, her colleagues would all be walking into Dupont's trap instead of the other way around. They'd be mousemeat, just like Dupont had promised. Gorgonzilla and Muenster the Monster would feast on their flesh, and Brie de Sorbonne would have a whole new wardrobe to take home to Paris.

My first Silver Skateboard mission is a total bust, thought Glory wretchedly. *I'm a failure.* Bunsen was right, it was her pride that was to blame. It had got her – had got them all – into this horrible fix. Her stupid Goldenleaf pride.

Glory slumped under the bench, exhausted and demoralized and more scared than she'd ever been in her whole young mouse life. The parade was going to be a disaster, they were all going to die, the rats would take over the world and there was nothing she or anybody else could do to stop it.

She watched listlessly as across the room the mob

of rats fell upon their revolting feast with gusto. Mouldy orange rinds and stale sandwich crusts, half-eaten cookies and half-empty cartons of sour milk – everything a rat needed for a party. Glory turned away in revulsion.

'Eat up, my friends!' cried Dupont, licking the last few drops of leftover Slurpie from a styrofoam cup. 'We move out at dawn.'

CHAPTER
TWENTY-SEVEN

DAY THREE – THURSDAY 0830 HOURS

'How come whenever I'm with you, I always end up in some dumb costume?' grumbled DB. 'Sheesh. This is worse than the apron *and* the donkey suit combined.'

Oz was wrestling with the silver buckle on the belt of his pilgrim-boy suit, which was at least one size too small. He glanced over at DB. She was wearing a long black pilgrim-girl dress, complete with white apron and white hat. He sighed. 'You're right. We look ridiculous.'

The Mayflower Flour man strode into the gilded lobby of the Waldorf-Astoria, where the winners of the bake-off had gathered to await the arrival of their limousine. Lavinia Levinson and Amelia Bean were seated on one of the fancy sofas, discussing cheese twists with Mary Lou Swenson of Oshkosh, Wisconsin. Jordan, dressed as a bag of Mayflower Flour, and Tank, who had been stuffed reluctantly into an enormous pumpkin costume, were posing sullenly for yet another picture.

'Doesn't Sherman look adorable!' exclaimed Mrs Wilson to Mrs Scott. 'And your Jordan, too. They're growing up so fast!'

The Mayflower Flour man clapped his hands. 'Winners! We need you in the limo now! At the double! The parade is starting soon!'

A blast of cold air struck Oz as the group was herded out of the lobby. It was perfect Thanksgiving weather, clear as a bell – but it was bitterly cold. *At least the pilgrim-boy suit is wool*, he thought, shivering. He climbed gratefully into the warmth of the limousine, which whisked them up Park Avenue towards Central Park and West Seventy-seventh Street.

Oz glanced out of the window as they passed the park. Most of the trees were bare by now, their branches stark against the bright blue November sky. A few were still decked in a late autumn palette of faded russet and brown, and here and there a scattering of bright yellow leaves clung to the branches, stirring like golden coins in the light breeze.

The limousine came to a halt, and the chauffeur leaped from the car and opened the rear door smartly. The adults got out first, and next it was Oz's turn. As he heaved himself awkwardly across the low-slung leather seat, Jordan poked him in the back.

'Could you swim a little faster, whale boy?'

The chauffeur reached in and hauled Oz bodily out.

'Thanks,' Oz mumbled, red-faced. For about the millionth time in his life, Oz wished that he was James Bond. Riding in a limousine was no big deal to Agent 007. When the superspy wasn't driving fast sports cars, he rode in limousines all the time. But, then, James Bond didn't need help getting *out* of a limousine. James Bond wasn't built like a baby whale.

'There's the float!' cried Amelia Bean as Oz emerged, followed by her daughter. 'Isn't it a beauty!'

The base of the Mayflower Flour float was a small replica of Plymouth Harbor, complete with painted sea and a fake Plymouth Rock to represent where America's first settlers had stepped ashore. Tethered to this by four sturdy ropes and bobbing gently in the breeze was a gigantic fully rigged

197

balloon ship, with *Mayflower* painted on its side.

'Wow!' said DB, and even Jordan and Tank looked dazzled.

'Isn't this exciting, kids?' said Lavinia Levinson, her voice brimming with enthusiasm. 'I just knew you'd win!'

Mayflower Flour had persuaded Oz's mother to provide some entertainment during the parade, and she was humming the medley of seasonal music she'd chosen to warm up the crowd. Amelia Bean, of course, was busy filming everything with her camcorder.

Oz and DB exchanged a glance. Their mothers were far more excited than they were. But, then again, their mothers would be safe down on the float. Their mothers didn't have to ride on the balloon ship with a pair of sharks.

A Mayflower Flour employee dressed as a Native American helped them up on to the float, and then propped a ladder alongside the ship. Oz, DB, Jordan, Tank and Mary Lou Swenson of Oshkosh, Wisconsin, climbed aboard it. Down below, 'ashore' on the float's base, the four mothers waved.

'Smile for the camera, Shermie!' squealed Mrs Wilson. 'My little pumpkin!'

'You are so dead, Fatboy,' promised Tank through teeth gritted in a smile.

Oz ignored him. He was determined not to react. Reacting only got the sharks all worked up. James Bond never reacted. James Bond was always as cool as a cucumber. *I am as cool as a cucumber,* Oz told himself sternly, but he couldn't help eyeing Tank and Jordan with suspicion. The sixth graders were whispering to themselves, clearly up to something.

'Duck!' shouted Tank, as a pigeon swooped low overhead. He and Jordan dived for cover. Oz looked up just in time to catch the small scroll of paper that dropped from the sky.

'What was that?' cried Jordan.

Oz shrugged, pocketing the note. 'I didn't see anything,' he said. He jerked his chin at DB and, as everyone took their places below (the Mayflower Flour man positioned Lavinia Levinson smack dab on top of Plymouth Rock), the two of them moved a safe distance away from the others. Oz unrolled the note and squinted at it. He'd forgotten to tuck the magnifying glass in the pocket of his pilgrim-boy suit.

'H and A,' he whispered, giving DB the key to the code.

She twirled the rings on the cipher disk until they

were in the proper place. 'Fire away,' she told him.

As Oz read aloud the sequence of letters, DB decoded the message. 'FOR YOUR PAWS ONLY,' she whispered. 'LOST COMMUNICATION WITH GLORY, BUT MISSION STILL HAS GREEN LIGHT. SEE YOU IN TIMES SQUARE!'

Jordan's head popped up over Oz's shoulder. 'Watcha got there?' he demanded.

'Um, nothing,' said Oz, prodding at his glasses. He scrunched up the note in his hand, but Jordan grabbed his hand and Tank prised open his fingers one by one until he finally managed to rip the note from his grasp.

The sharks stared at tiny slip of paper. 'Look, Tank, it's a teeny tiny message! In code.'

'Aw, isn't that cute,' Tank replied. 'Dogbones and Fatboy are playing spy.' He looked Oz up and down, his gaze settling on the too-tight belt around the middle of his too-tight pilgrim-boy suit. He smirked. 'Except you don't look much like 007 to me.'

'More like BLUBBER-O-SEVEN!' said Jordan, and the two boys hooted.

Oz reddened again. A gust of wind blew across

the park and set the ship rocking to and fro on its moorings. He started to feel seasick. It was shaping up to be another long morning.

CHAPTER
TWENTY-EIGHT

DAY THREE – THURSDAY 0845 HOURS

On the underside of the Mayflower Flour float, Glory shivered as the blast of cold wind hit her too.

'I'm freezing,' whined Limburger Lulu.

The rats huddled closer together, and Glory shrank back, wrinkling her nose in disgust. The smell was almost overpowering.

At first light, her captors had left the dinosaur exhibit and

crept down to the subway stop beneath the museum. From there, they'd proceeded to the corner of West Seventy-seventh and Columbus Avenue, emerging on to the street through a sewer grating directly beneath the Mayflower Flour float. Not a soul had seen them stow away; not a soul would be able to warn the mice of the impending disaster.

'So when do the festivities commence?' growled Stilton Piccadilly.

'"When do the festivities commence?"' mimicked Dupont in a fake British accent. 'What's the matter with you, Stilton? Can't you speak English? Just spit it out. This is New York, pal – there are no "festivities" here. Just a Big Apple-sized party! A shindig! A bash!'

Glory felt the British rodent tense up beside her. The rats were hungry – they'd postponed breakfast until after the parade – and a hungry rat was a mean rat.

'Things should be starting any minute now,' Mozzarella Canal said soothingly, stepping in between the two rivals. 'Been coming to this parade since I was a ratling. You're in for a real treat, boys, I promise you. Breakfast may be late, but just wait until you see what the street vendors leave behind!'

Distracted by the mention of food, his nephew's

eyes shone greedily. 'Hotdogs. Pretzels. Honey-roasted nuts,' Mozzarella said, and Dupont groaned at the mere thought of the feast that awaited. 'Italian sausage and hot chestnuts too.' A slimy trickle of drool appeared at the corner of Dupont's mouth.

Revolted, Glory averted her eyes. She hunched miserably in the chill November air. She was cold, she was surrounded by rats – including at least two mousivores – and everything had gone horribly, horribly wrong. Even now, all of her colleagues would be moving into place. They had no idea that Dupont and his smorgasbord of long-tailed gluttons were one step ahead of them. By the time the mice came aboard in Times Square, it would be too late. She'd be mousemeat, and the Global Rodent Roundtable would be poised to take over the world. With Fumble's help.

Glory glared at her traitorous colleague. Her paws itched to reach over and slap his smug face. Except they were still tied behind her. Dupont had gagged her again, too. Fumble! Minister of Mouse Affairs, indeed. Minister of Back-stabbers was more like it.

Glory had stayed awake all night, worrying about what would happen with a mole like Fumble in place. He'd feed information to the rats about secret missions and secret agents, and the Spy Mice Agency network would crumble within weeks. Days, maybe. After that, the rest of her familiar world would quickly follow. Even with the protection of the Mouse Guard, the guilds didn't have enough resources to hold out for long against literate rats. Or against treachery of the very highest order.

The float gave a lurch as the truck attached to the front of it roared to life.

'This is it!' Dupont cried, his harsh voice barely audible above the noise of the engine. 'In a few minutes, we'll give the mice a taste of rat power the likes of which they've never seen before! In a few minutes, the world will know the name Roquefort Dupont – and all the rest of you,' he added hastily, waving a paw at the other delegates.

'MICE-FREE FROM SEA TO SEA! MICE-FREE FOR YOU AND ME!' chanted Limburger Lulu and Limburger Louie.

Dupont looked over at Glory. He drew a claw across his throat and grinned, revealing his sharp yellow fangs. 'Times Square, here we come!'

Glory's tail trembled. Times Square. Where time would run out for her – permanently. There'd be no B-Nut and Bunsen to rescue her this time around.

Dear, sweet, loyal Bunsen! The thought of her friend was almost too much for Glory, and she sniffled remorsefully. Bunsen didn't deserve a fate like this. Especially not a fate that her pride had caused.

Stiffen your tail, Agent Goldenleaf, she told herself. Fear and terror, her father had told her a long time ago, were a rat's best weapons. And her weapon – the only one left to her at this point – was courage. She was going to need every ounce she could muster. What was it that Julius had said? Calm, cool, clear thinking. Yes. She would need that, too. With any luck, Dupont might just make a mistake. And if he did, she wanted to be ready for it.

The distant drums grew closer as a marching band approached, signalling the start of the parade. Above them on the float there was a sudden flurry of activity – human voices calling out and human feet thudding to and fro as the balloon ship's tethers were checked and everyone took their places.

Glory's ears pricked up as she recognized Oz's voice. He was so close! If only she could get his attention! She glanced around frantically. But she was still surrounded by rats, still gagged, her paws still tied behind her. She'd have to bide her time.

The float gave another lurch as the truck continued

forward and turned on to Central Park West. The humans thronging the pavements began to cheer as the giant balloon ship set sail.

'Get ready, gang,' cried Dupont jubilantly. 'This party is about to begin!'

CHAPTER
TWENTY-NINE

DAY THREE - THURSDAY 0930 HOURS

High up on the deck of the Mayflower Flour balloon ship, Oz smiled and waved.

He'd never seen so many people in his entire life. Not even the Fourth of July on the Washington Mall was this crowded. People lined the pavements; people leaned out of windows in office buildings and apartment buildings and hotels; people crowded on to steps and into store fronts, shinnied up traffic lights and lamp posts and flagpoles, and clambered up construction scaffolding – anything for a better view of the parade. Everyone was bundled up against the chilly November air, but it was sunny and people were smiling and laughing and clearly excited to see the parade finally get under way.

From his vantage point, Oz could see for streets and streets. There were clowns – hundreds of clowns! – and cheerleaders, choirs and marching bands. Majorettes in spangled costumes twirled their batons, brass bands blasted their music and costumed creatures cavorted on stilts and unicycles. There were kilted pipers and policemen on horseback, and even a forest of tap-dancing trees. Toddlers on their fathers' shoulders gaped at the floats – a castle, a fake tram car, an even bigger fake river paddle steamer. And then there were the balloons! The highlight of the procession, they were spread out as far as the eye could see, some of them six storeys tall. As the parade glided down Manhattan's normally traffic-packed streets, Oz noted that the *Mayflower* was slotted in between a big smiling sponge and an enormous green frog balloon.

'LADIES AND GENTLEPILGRIMS!' cried the Mayflower Flour man into a microphone as the giant balloon ship rounded Columbus Circle and turned down Broadway. The crowd roared with excitement, momentarily drowning him out.

'I PRESENT TO YOU THIS YEAR'S WINNERS OF THE TWENTY-FIFTH ANNUAL MAYFLOWER FLOUR BAKE-OFF! FOR HER CHEESE TWISTS, MARY LOU SWENSON OF OSHKOSH, WISCONSIN! AND IN THE JUNIOR DIVISION, FOR THEIR PUMPKIN CHOC-OLATE-CHIP BREAD, DELILAH BEAN AND OZYMANDIAS LEVINSON OF WASH-INGTON DC!'

The crowd roared its approval once again and tens of thousands of cameras winked and flashed. *Great,* thought Oz, who was more than a little sensitive about the fact that his parents had named him after a poem by the English poet Shelley. *Now the whole world knows my real name.*

A cluster of Mayflower Flour employees dressed as pilgrims and Native Americans scurried to the edges of the float and began tossing cheese twists and slices of pumpkin chocolate-chip bread to the onlookers. As the crowd scrambled for the treats, the Mayflower Flour man lifted his microphone once again.

'AND NOW, FOR YOUR LISTENING PLEASURE, IT'S MY GREAT HONOUR TO

INTRODUCE THAT DELECTABLE DIVA HERSELF, THE ONE, THE ONLY, LAVINIA LEVINSON!'

Perched on Plymouth Rock, Oz's mother raised her arms dramatically, as if to embrace the city itself. The crowd went wild. Nodding to her accompanist at the keyboard, who was dressed as the Thanksgiving turkey, she swung into her first set of tunes. Amelia Bean scrambled forward to record the moment on film.

DB leaned over to Oz. 'Your mom's good,' she said, shouting to be heard above the music.

'I know,' Oz shouted back proudly. Out of the corner of his eye, he saw Jordan whisper something to Tank. Oz nudged DB. 'Check it out,' he said, nodding towards the boys. 'The sharks are up to something.'

Jordan and Tank grinned and gave them a big thumbs-up. DB's eyes narrowed. 'No kidding,' she replied. 'Keep your eyes peeled.'

The float sailed on down Broadway. In the distance, Oz could make out the huge neon billboards that were the icons of Times Square, where he knew Bunsen and B-Nut and the other spy mice would join them. Once his colleagues were aboard, they'd all take their positions for pouncing on the rats, who, thanks to the misinformation Glory had planted in her bold move last night, were expecting to ambush them in front of Macy's in Herald Square.

Oz hummed along to the music, waving to the crowd and enjoying the spectacle. Despite the presence of the sharks, he was feeling happy this morning. He wasn't a loser after all. In fact, he had a blue ribbon to prove it. And in a short while, he'd have another successful mission for the Spy Mice Agency under his belt.

Oz was so busy enjoying himself that neither he nor DB – nor any other human, for that matter – noticed a long snout emerge from behind the fake bushes lining the fake Plymouth shore. The snout snuffled at the contents of a large basket sitting in front of the fake bushes. A cheese twist suddenly flipped up out of the basket and disappeared into the fake bushes as the snout snapped it out of sight.

The first set of tunes came to a close, and the Mayflower Flour man once again stepped up to the mike. 'LET'S HEAR IT FOR LAVINIA LEVINSON!' he cried. The crowd applauded and cheered. He held up a bag of Mayflower Flour. 'AND

REMEMBER, FOLKS, YOUR SHIP ALWAYS COMES IN WHEN YOU BAKE WITH MAYFLOWER FLOUR!'

Across the deck on the balloon ship, Jordan and Tank both held up bags of Mayflower Flour, too. The crowd cheered again, and Lavinia Levinson bowed graciously and swung into another festive medley.

'Uh-oh,' said Oz, realizing too late what his classmates were up to. Before he and DB could duck out of the way, Jordan and Tank rushed forward and dumped the contents of the bags over their heads.

'I HEREBY CROWN YOU FATBOY AND DOGBONES, KING AND QUEEN OF THE BAKE-OFF!' cried Jordan. The crowd exploded with laughter. Assuming their applause and cheers were for the music, no one on the float below noticed the antics above them on the *Mayflower*.

'You – you – *morons*!' sputtered DB, flailing at the cloud of white that engulfed her.

Oz was coughing too hard to say anything.

'Watcha gonna do about it?' taunted Jordan. 'Set your hamster on us?'

The boys strutted about in a victory dance. They bowed to the delighted crowd. As Oz struggled to wipe the flour from his face, a movement at the far edge of the deck caught his eye. It was a cheese twist. A cheese twist moving across the ship all by itself. *By itself?* thought Oz. *Wait a minute.* He shook his head, releasing a whirlwind of flour, and looked again. He grabbed blindly for DB's arm. The cheese twist was not all by itself. Attached to one end of it was none other than Roquefort Dupont.

'What?' DB turned to look at him.

'Uh,' croaked Oz. He stared down Broadway. They were still streets away from Times Square. Something wasn't right – the rats weren't supposed to show up yet. Not until Macy's. Had plans changed? If so, he and DB hadn't been informed. He peered up at the sky. There wasn't a pigeon – or a spy mouse – in sight.

'Something's wrong,' he said, coughing puffs of flour.

'You better believe something's wrong,' DB replied crossly, flapping her braids. 'It's in my hair. How come everything always ends up in my hair?'

Oz tugged on her sleeve. 'DB,' he whispered urgently, still choking on flour. 'DB, something's *really* wrong. The rats are here.'

'I know the rats are here!' said DB. 'You don't have to tell me that! Two big rats named Jordan

214

and Tank! I have had enough of those jerks!'

Oz shook his head, releasing another cascade of flour. He prodded at his glasses with a pudgy finger, trying to wipe the lenses clean but only managing to smear them with white. 'That's not what I meant,' he said, pointing across the deck to where Dupont was crouched behind a fake sea chest, greedily tucking into his stolen treat. Over the edge of the deck, another set of whiskers appeared and then another. The rats were gathering.

'Holy smokes,' said DB. 'What are they doing here? We're nowhere near Macy's!'

Oz spotted a small heap of brown fur at the feet of Roquefort Dupont. He stiffened.

'What?' asked DB in alarm.

'They've got Glory!'

DB gasped. Oz looked around wildly for a weapon. There was nothing in sight. Bending over, he wrenched his heavy black pilgrim shoe off his foot, held it up menacingly, and started towards Dupont.

The big grey rat stood up on his hindpaws as Oz approached. He stared at him with his red, glowing eyes. A malicious smile appeared beneath his ugly snout.

'Oz, don't,' called DB. 'Wait for the mice.'

'It'll be too late for Glory if I do,' Oz replied.

Still grinning, Dupont reached down and plucked Glory from the *Mayflower*'s deck with one powerful sweep of his paw. He dangled her by the neck, several centimetres above the balloon deck's surface. He began to squeeze. Oz watched in horror as Glory struggled, her tiny legs kicking frantically.

'Oz, back off!' cried DB. 'Now!'

Oz hesitated. He lowered his shoe. Dupont watched him, still squeezing. Oz took a step backwards. Sneering, Dupont released Glory. She crumpled to the deck in a heap.

'Dupont's got us trapped,' said Oz to DB, his round face red with fury. 'If we try and rescue Glory, he'll kill her.'

'But we can't just stand here and do nothing!'

'I don't intend to do nothing,' said Oz grimly. 'Put your headset on and wait here.'

He ran to the deck railing and heaved himself over it, teetering on the balloon's edge. The ladder that they'd used to climb aboard had been taken away and strapped to the truck pulling the float. Oz looked down. It was a long drop to Plymouth Harbor. He swallowed hard. He had to do it; he had no choice. He had to alert his colleagues that their plan had gone awry. He had to save Glory.

What I need is a parachute, thought Oz. Agent 007 always carried a parachute. He closed his eyes and made a wish. He opened them again. No parachute. *Here goes nothing,* he thought, jamming on his headset.

'The name is Levinson, Oz Levinson,' he muttered under his breath, and jumped.

DB shrieked as her classmate plummeted downwards. For a split second Oz thought it was all over. But the side of the *Mayflower* sloped outwards just enough to catch him, and he slid the rest of the way down to Plymouth's shore, leaving a long smudge of white flour trailing behind him. Lurching to his feet, he lumbered across the float towards his mother.

Lavinia Levinson's eyes widened in surprise when she saw her flour-coated son. But she was a diva, and divas didn't miss a beat. She held up a finger, signalling Oz to wait a moment, and quickly brought her song to a graceful conclusion.

The Mayflower Flour man stepped forward, frowned at Oz, and took the microphone from his mother. He began to address the crowd again, extolling the virtues of Mayflower Flour.

'Oz, what on earth happened to you?' Oz's mother

asked, crouching down beside him.

'It's a long story,' Oz replied. 'Mom, I need your help.'

'Sure, sweetie, anything. Those boys bothering you? I'll take care of that so fast it'll make their heads spin.' She cast a fierce glance over at Jordan and Tank's mothers, who were waving to the crowd, oblivious to the commotion. Amelia Bean had her back to them, too, busily filming the tap-dancing trees that preceded them in the parade line-up.

'It's not that. Remember the song you recorded for DB and me? Back in our hotel room?'

'"Born to Shake My Tail"?'

Oz nodded. 'I need you to sing it.'

His mother gaped at him in astonishment. 'Now? Here?'

'Yes,' said Oz. 'It's really, really important.'

Lavinia Levinson chewed her lip. 'Really?'

Oz nodded again, and tears welled up in his eyes. Glory's life hung in the balance. But there was no way he could explain that to his mother. He just didn't have time.

His mother saw the tears and gave his floury hand a squeeze. 'OK,' she whispered. She glanced up

218

towards the balloon ship's deck. Jordan and Tank grinned and waved. Lavinia Levinson scowled. 'Remember,' she said to Oz, '"It ain't over . . ."'

A smile tugged at the corner of her son's mouth. '"Till the fat lady sings",' he replied, completing their lifelong 'I love you' ritual.

Lavinia Levinson straightened up again. She plucked the microphone from the startled Mayflower Flour man, silencing him mid-sentence. He didn't protest, however. Sometimes it paid to be a diva. She crossed the float to the Thanksgiving turkey, whispered something to him and hummed a few bars. Her accompanist nodded. His hands hovered over the keyboard, then descended to strike the opening notes of 'Born to Shake My Tail'.

Up on the *Mayflower*'s deck, the half-strangled heap of fur that was Glory stirred slightly. Her elegant little ears perked up. That music! There was something familiar about it. Could it be . . .? She shook her head wearily and closed her eyes. Impossible. She must be hallucinating.

'I'm a hard-rockin' mouse, and I bring down the house every time I twitch my tail!'

Glory opened her eyes. She sat up. She knew that music as well as she knew her own whiskers!

No doubt about it, she was listening to the Steel Acorns' number-one hit.

As 'Born to Shake My Tail' rang out down Broadway, sung by none other than world-famous opera star Lavinia Levinson, Glory's heart swelled with hope for the first time since her capture. If Bunsen and B-Nut heard this, they'd know something was up.

'Well done, Ozymandias Levinson,' Glory whispered softly, as the musical warning floated out across New York City. 'Well done, indeed.'

CHAPTER THIRTY

'Now!' cried Hotspur Folger as the Mayflower Flour float sailed into Times Square. He threw his gleaming silver skateboard down on the pavement and was all set to leap into action when Bunsen placed a paw on his shoulder.

'Wait,' said the lab mouse. 'Something's wrong.'

Bunsen had spent a restless night, worried about Glory. His pink eyes were ringed in dark circles, and his white fur was sticking up every which way.

Hotspur glared at him. 'Nothing's wrong,' he snapped. 'You need to learn to obey orders.'

Hotspur had lost no time taking over the mission in Glory's absence, and he wasn't about to let his shot at fame be derailed. To outsmart and eliminate

221

not only Dupont, but also every major rat in the world? It was a coup beyond imagining! A triumph! His picture would be on the cover of every magazine and newspaper! *Miceweek* would run a profile of him; the *Tattletail* would make up breathless rumours about his life. He'd be the talk of the town. With a bit of luck, he'd be running the Spy Mice Agency before long. Maybe even run for a seat on the Council. Yes, Hotspur Folger's future was bright with promise, and he was not about to let some insignificant little runt of a lab mouse ruin his plans.

'Slap your board down, soldier!' he shouted. 'It's time to kick some rat tail!'

Bunsen hesitated. Insubordination by a field agent was forbidden. A firing offence. But Bunsen's own ears were telling him something was wrong, and Bunsen couldn't ignore his own ears. He held his ground. 'Hotspur, listen to me. Don't you hear that music? *Something's wrong.*'

Hotspur cocked an ear towards the approaching float. So did Bubble and Squeak.

'"Born to Shake My Tail"!' gasped Squeak. 'Hotspur, he's right! Something's wrong!'

'What could be wrong?' Hotspur glowered. 'Everything's going exactly according to plan.'

Bunsen decided to take matters into his own paws. 'B-Nut, come in! B-Nut, come in!' he called into his tiny headset.

He stepped out from under the peanut vendor's cart at the junction of Forty-second Street and Broadway and looked up at the sky. Four pigeons were circling overhead. On their backs were B-Nut and the Steel Acorns, awaiting their part in the operation.

'You're coming through loud and clear, Bunsen,' B-Nut replied.

'Do you hear that music?'

'You bet I do.'

'Something's up.'

'No kidding. Let me do a quick recon and get back to you.'

'Born to dance! Born to wail! Born to shake my tail!' sang Lavinia Levinson. At the last phrase, she turned around and coyly wiggled her large bottom. The crowd cheered. They loved seeing the dignified diva cut loose.

'BRAVA!' they cried, picking up the refrain and wiggling their bottoms, too.

'BORN TO DANCE! BORN TO WAIL! BORN TO SHAKE MY TAIL!' everyone sang, as Times Square rocked to the beat of the Steel Acorns' number-one hit.

In all the commotion, no one noticed the lone pigeon who swooped low over the deck of the balloon ship and then circled back towards the corner of Forty-second and Broadway.

'Not good, gang,' B-Nut reported. 'Something's definitely gone wrong. The rats are already aboard.'

Bunsen stomach did a flip-flop. 'What about Glory?'

'She's with them,' replied B-Nut.

'Is she – is she all right?' asked Bunsen fearfully.

B-Nut was silent for a moment. 'Yeah, but she doesn't look so good. I'd try an aerial rescue, but there are too many rats. I'd never even get close.'

'The rats are all there?' Hotspur couldn't hide his excitement.

'Dozens of them,' said B-Nut. 'Dupont, Stilton, Brie, Gorgonzola – all the kingpins.'

Hotspur's eyes narrowed as he gazed up at the approaching balloon. 'Then we move the timetable forward. Cut it loose now.'

'*Now?*' asked Bubble. His normally calm voice was agitated. 'But I thought we weren't going to proceed with that until Herald Square?'

224

'Yes, that's right,' added Squeak. 'After the parade. When everyone is safely off the float.'

'We cut it loose now,' repeated Hotspur.

Bunsen stared at him in disbelief. 'Hotspur, Glory and the kids are still aboard!'

'Sacrifices have to be made in this business,' Hotspur replied coldly. 'You know that as well as I do. Have you forgotten our motto? *The noblest motive is the public good.*'

'No, I haven't forgotten our motto!' cried Bunsen, his nose and tail flaming red with outrage. 'But I haven't forgotten my friends, either! "To the last gasp with truth and loyalty", as the Bard says, or have *you* forgotten?'

'We cut the balloon loose now!' Hotspur said stubbornly. 'This is a once-in-a-lifetime chance! My uncle said so himself. We'll never have another shot at eliminating the entire leadership of the rat world.'

In reply, Bunsen gathered up his flamingo-pink skateboard. Glory's skateboard.

'Stand down, lab mouse,' ordered Hotspur.

'The heck I will, *Snotspur*!' Bunsen retorted.

'That's it!' screamed Hotspur. 'You just crossed the line, lab mouse! I'm going to make a note to report you!'

'Write it on your bicep, why don't you?' Bunsen screamed back. 'You look at it often enough!'

The two mice stood nose to nose. Hotspur glared at Bunsen. Bunsen's whiskers trembled, but he didn't back down. There was a steely glint in his normally gentle pink eyes. He was sick and tired of Hotspur and his insults. The mouse he loved was in danger, and he, Bunsen Burner, was determined to save her.

Hotspur flicked a glance towards the float, which was almost upon them. 'You've got five minutes,' he snapped.

'Good luck, Bunsen,' whispered Squeak, as he hopped on to his silver skateboard. 'We'll be right behind you.'

Bubble gave him a paws-up. 'If anyone can do it, you can, Mr Burner!'

As the float rumbled slowly past the corner of Forty-second and Broadway, Bunsen shoved off with a hindpaw and scooted out into the street. Hotspur and the two British agents followed close on his tail. The crowd was too busy dancing and singing to notice them, and the mice whizzed underneath the float undetected.

Whipping out their harpoon pens, they each took

aim at the passing float. Four strands of dental floss flew upwards; four sharpened pen nibs snagged on the underside of the float's trailer. Moving as one, the mice flipped their boards up and into their backpacks, then climbed paw over paw up their lines of floss, creeping over the side of the float to emerge in a clump of fake bushes.

'B-Nut, Acorns, wait for my signal,' Hotspur commanded. 'I'm giving Bunsen a five-minute head start, then we'll cut the tethers.'

'Got it,' B-Nut replied, as Bunsen scampered past the basket of cheese twists towards the balloon ship.

'Dude, what's wrong with Oz and DB?' asked Romeo from his perch far above, on Ollie's back. 'Check it out – they're as white as Bunsen.'

The mice stared at the children. Oz was still standing by his mother. DB was still up on the *Mayflower*'s deck, leaning over the rail. Bunsen sped across the float and sniffed the white trail Oz had left on the balloon ship's side.

'Flour,' he reported into his headset. 'Someone dumped flour on them.'

'Gotta be the sharks!' cried Lip.

'Right,' B-Nut replied. 'Acorns, we've got five

227

minutes. I say it's time for a little payback, spy mice-style.'

'Rock on, dude!' cried Nutmeg.

'Hold your positions!' ordered Hotspur angrily, but the rocker mice and their surveillance-pilot leader ignored him. Instead, they urged their pigeons forward towards Jordan and Tank.

'Target in range,' squawked Hank.

'Ready?' called B-Nut.

'Ready!' replied the Acorns.

'Aim!'

The pigeons circled low.

'Fire!'

The pigeons dropped their loads.

'EEEEEEWWWWWW!' cried the boys, as a shower of pigeon poo splatted down on them from the sky above.

Jordan swiped at his face frantically. 'THIS IS DISGUSTING!' he hollered.

'MOMMY!' wailed Tank.

'Right tool for the right job,' said B-Nut in satisfaction. 'Julius would be proud, boys. Let's go in for another pass!'

Hank and the other pigeons circled again and repeated the manoeuvre. In a short time, Jordan and Tank were nearly as covered in white as DB and Oz.

Still rocking and rolling to the beat of 'Born to Shake My Tail', the crowd only slowly began to notice what was going on. A roar of laughter went up, and once again thousands of cameras winked and flashed. Then the TV cameras zoomed in. To Jordan and Tank's horror, their stricken, pigeon poo-covered faces suddenly appeared on Times Square's giant TV screen and billboards, from there to be transmitted via satellite to television sets around the world.

'I do not believe I am seeing this,' said Amelia Bean to Lavinia Levinson.

'And you thought Hallowe'en was bad!' crowed DB. 'Go, Acorns!'

Oz was laughing so hard he fell helplessly to the ground. 'What goes around, comes around,' he wheezed, clutching the sides of his flour-coated pilgrim-boy suit.

With the crowd distracted by the music and the shark sideshow, Hotspur, Bubble and Squeak split up, each heading for one of the sturdy rope tethers that anchored the balloon ship to the float. Moving with clockwork precision, they pulled out their lapel knives and stood poised at the ready.

'NOW!' cried Hotspur, as Bunsen scampered up the fourth tether towards the ship's deck.

Bubble and Squeak exchanged a worried glance. 'But you said five minutes!' Squeak protested.

'Close enough,' Hotspur replied, and began to saw.

Bubble defiantly resheathed his blade. So did Squeak. 'Bunsen!' she called into her headset, trying to warn him. 'Bunsen, watch –'

Her transmission went dead. Squeak tapped her headset and looked over at Hotspur. He was fiddling with the master control on his transmitter. He'd switched their frequency! The two British agents watched in horror as he began to saw at the rope again. High above them, Bunsen tumbled unwittingly on to the *Mayflower*'s deck, landing at DB's feet.

'Bunsen! Am I glad to see you!' she said in relief. 'Dupont's got Glory.'

'I know,' said Bunsen. 'Abandon ship!'

'What?' said DB.

'Abandon ship!' Bunsen repeated. 'Get everyone off! This ship's due to sail.'

DB glanced around wildly. 'Sail?' she asked, bewildered. 'Where?'

'Just do it, Agent Bean,' barked Bunsen.

'ABANDON SHIP! That's an order.'

DB ran towards Mary Lou Swenson, who was trying to help wipe the pigeon poo off Jordan and Tank. As she tugged on the woman's coat sleeve, Bunsen pulled a single match and a table-tennis ball from his backpack and started towards Glory. He halted in his tracks, spotting Fumble. His pink eyes widened in surprise. The plump mouse saw him at the same moment. Smirking, he reached out and tugged on Dupont's tail.

In a flash, Bunsen understood what Glory had been trying to warn them about in her last transmission. 'MMM-MM,' she'd mumbled. Fumble, she'd been trying to say. *Their colleague was a traitor!* Bunsen stood rooted to the spot, his head spinning. It was inconceivable! No mouse would betray his own kind! What should he do?

Calm, cool, clear thinking, Julius always counselled. Bunsen took a deep breath and willed himself to concentrate. Glory's life was at stake, and her rescue would require split-second timing. He lit the match.

Across the deck, Dupont spun around. He cuffed Fumble, who cringed, then pointed at Bunsen.

'Here, Dupont – catch!' the lab mouse cried,

231

igniting the table-tennis ball and rolling it towards the rodent.

A puff of smoke burst from the tiny bomb just as it reached Dupont, enveloping him in a cloud. Using the smoke for cover, Bunsen raced towards Glory. He'd almost reached her when Hotspur's tether gave way. The deck gave a sudden lurch, and the table-tennis ball started rolling back towards Bunsen.

'NO!' cried the lab mouse. It hadn't been five minutes yet – Hotspur had double-crossed him!

The deck tilted sharply, and DB, Mary Lou Swenson, Jordan and Tank slid towards the rail. They screamed. So did everyone on the float below. Bunsen whipped his harpoon pen out of his backpack and shot a line of floss into the fake sea chest, then hung on for dear life.

The crowd in Times Square sensed something happening and began to back away from the float. On its base, the Mayflower Flour man ran around in a panic. 'Get the ladder!' he cried.

But it was too late for the ladder. Unable to bear the strain of the enormous balloon ship, a second tether snapped. The *Mayflower* tilted almost vertically, and DB, Mary Lou Swenson and the two pigeon poo-covered sixth graders slid under the rail and

232

down the ship's side, landing in a heap in the fake Plymouth Harbor. Dupont, who was clutching Glory, scrabbled wildly for a claw-hold. So did the rest of the rats.

The third tether gave way with a snap as loud as a gunshot, and the crowd screamed. The *Mayflower* bobbed in the air, anchored to the float now only by a single rope.

'Oz!' cried DB. 'Do something! Bunsen and Glory are still aboard!'

Oz swiped frantically at his glasses. He peered up to see Bunsen, who had clipped the strand of dental floss through the karabiner on his utility belt, hauling himself paw over paw towards his true love.

'Hang on!' Oz cried. 'I'm coming!' He ran forward and flung himself bodily at the fourth tether. It groaned, straining mightily at its mooring.

'Look out!' shrieked the Thanksgiving turkey. 'It's gonna give!'

'Oz!' bellowed Lavinia Levinson, her well-trained voice carrying above the terrified screams of the crowd. 'Get away from there!'

Oz ignored her. 'Bunsen! Glory!' he called again, clinging tightly to the rope.

'Abandon ship!' screeched Dupont, finally releasing

233

Glory to save himself. As a stream of rodents began heading for the fourth tether, she plummeted down across the tilted deck, straight into Bunsen's paws. The crowd spotted the rats and screamed even louder.

'OZ!' hollered his mother. 'LET GO OF THAT ROPE!'

Above him, Oz could see his two friends clinging desperately to each other. He flinched as Scurvy scampered down the tether and over his arm and back, but he didn't let go. He was determined not to let go until Bunsen and Glory were safe.

'Hurry!' he called.

Claws scrabbled in Oz's hair and along his body as the delegates of the Global Rodent Roundtable began to flee like rats fleeing the proverbial sinking ship. Gnaw was next, then the Limburger twins. Oz watched helplessly as Brie shoved Gorgonzola out of her way and slid determinedly towards his head.

On the deck above, Glory looked at Bunsen. 'Sacrifices must be made,' she said calmly.

Bunsen gazed back sorrowfully into her bright little eyes. 'The noblest motive is the public good,' he replied.

Glory leaned in towards the lab mouse's headset and flipped its setting to Oz and DB's frequency. 'Let go of the rope, Oz!' she called, her voice barely audible above the pandemonium.

'No!' cried Oz, flinching as another rat crawled down the length of his body. 'I can't do it!'

'Now, Oz!' ordered Glory.

'What about you?' he wailed.

'Oz, this is a direct order,' shouted Glory, her small voice ringing with authority. 'LET GO OF THE ROPE!'

With a sob, Oz opened his hands and released the tether. He flopped backwards on to the float. The tether gave another mighty groan and then – CRACK! – it split in two. The *Mayflower* snapped upright, sending Dupont and the other rats tumbling back on to the deck with Bunsen and Glory.

A hush fell over Times Square. Thousands of parade-goers watched in silence as the *Mayflower*, suddenly released from all that held it earthbound, spun about between the tall buildings for a long moment as if unsure of what to do. And then, a brisk wind blew down Broadway, filling its sails.

Oz watched helplessly as the ship, carrying his doomed friends, sailed off into the bright blue November sky.

CHAPTER
THIRTY-ONE

DAY THREE – THURSDAY 1015 HOURS

'You got us into this!' Stilton Piccadilly screamed at Dupont as the remainder of the Global Rodent Roundtable swirled around the *Mayflower*'s deck in a panic, frantically seeking some means of escape. 'You and your blasted books! "Reading rats will rule the world!" you said. "Reading rats are the rats of the future!" Rubbish! Forget books – this should have been about claws and jaws from the very start.'

'Claws and jaws?' Roquefort Dupont glared at his rival. 'I'll show you claws and jaws, you pompous –'

'You're not fit to be Big Cheese!' snarled Piccadilly. 'I hereby remove you from office!' He lunged at Dupont.

'This is no time to be arguing!' Mozzarella Canal thrust himself between the two bull rats. 'We need to find a way out of this mess!'

Dupont eyed his rival coldly. 'I'll deal with you later,' he promised.

'I'll be waiting,' replied the British rat, with equal frostiness.

Dupont stalked over to where Glory and Bunsen sat, tied together with dental floss. 'Blame me, will he?' he muttered under his rancid breath. 'That no good, conniving, treacherous piece of –'

Glory couldn't resist. 'Rat scum?'

Dupont slashed at her with his tail. 'Shut your mousetrap!' he screeched. 'If anyone's to blame, it's you! In fact, if I had any sense at all, I'd give you the heave-ho right now! You too, pale face!' He grabbed the two mice by the scruff of their necks and dangled them over the edge of the deck. Bunsen peered down, gulped and quickly closed his eyes. It was a long, long way to terra firma.

Dupont jerked them back and flung them down

237

on deck. 'However,' he said with a note of regret, 'I did promise Brie and the others that they could have their fun.'

'I'm not sure I like the sound of that,' Bunsen said cautiously, as Dupont waddled off. 'What did he mean by "fun"?'

Glory shook her head. 'You don't want to know.' The end, when it came, was not going to be pretty. No point telling Bunsen he was going to finish up as a rat snack and slippers.

Together, the two mice watched as their balloon ship sailed down Broadway, soared past Macy's in Herald Square and headed straight for the Empire State Building.

There was a flurry of activity on the other side of the deck. They looked over to see Dupont and the other rats cobbling together what looked like a long lasso out of bits of broken tether and dental floss.

'What are they doing?' whispered Glory, as the mob of rodents heaved their creation overboard.

'I think they're going to try and anchor us to the Empire State Building,' Bunsen replied. 'The tower mast was originally planned as a docking station for dirigibles.'

'Dirigibles?'

'Airships. Zeppelins. You know, like the *Hindenburg*.'

Glory nodded, then swayed against Bunsen as the *Mayflower*, caught in the currents of air that eddied around the famous New York landmark, bumped into its top.

'Now, chaps!' roared Stilton Piccadilly, peering over the edge of the deck. 'Swing it around quickly!'

The G.R.R. members raced to manoeuvre their makeshift lasso. 'That's it!' Dupont cried. 'We've got it!'

The rats gave a great shout of triumph and hustled to tie down the line. 'As soon as she's stable, we'll ditch this tub,' Dupont said.

Glory nudged Bunsen. 'Look!' she whispered. In the distance, a small flock of pigeons was approaching. They were still a few streets away but they were gaining ground quickly. B-Nut and the Acorns were closing in on them. There was still hope for rescue!

Glory wriggled her paws together frantically behind her back in an effort to release her dental-floss bonds. 'Come on, Bunsen,' she urged, 'we have to be ready for them!'

She swayed against the lab mouse again as a gust of wind caught the *Mayflower*'s sails. The balloon ship creaked and groaned, tugging mightily against the slender lasso that anchored it to the skyscraper.

'Grab that rope!' cried Picadilly. 'Don't let go!'

But even the strength of six-dozen rats was no match for Mother Nature and, as the *Mayflower* was struck by another gusty blast, the lasso gave way. The rats screamed in frustration, and Bunsen and Glory fell silent as their only hope of rescue was quickly left behind.

The balloon ship sailed on over the triangular Flatiron Building, past Greenwich Village and Soho and the sad place where the Twin Towers of the World Trade Center had once crowned New York's skyline. It soared through the skyscraper canyons of lower Manhattan and on towards where the East River and the Hudson flowed into the harbour. In the distance, the Statue of Liberty lifted her torch in eternal salute.

As they passed over the dock where the Staten Island ferry was berthed, another gust of wind shot the *Mayflower* forward, out to sea.

Glory turned to Bunsen. 'I want to thank you for trying to rescue me,' she said. 'It was very brave of you. I'm just sorry it turned out this way.'

Bunsen ducked his head modestly. 'It was nothing.'

'I should have known Hotspur would try to dump me like so much garbage,' said Glory in disgust. 'Double-crossing slimeball.'

'I thought you liked Hotspur!' Bunsen replied, looking up in surprise. 'All those muscles! All that Shakespeare! He's such a mouse of action, so bold, so dashing, so –'

'Arrogant?' offered Glory. She shook her head. 'No, Bunsen, there's only one mouse for me.'

'There is?' A tendril of hope sprang up in the lab mouse's heart.

'Mmm hmm,' said Glory, smiling shyly at him.

A tide of joy surged through Bunsen. 'Really?' he cried. 'You mean it?'

Glory nodded.

'I feel ten centimetres tall!' Bunsen crowed. With a mighty wriggle, he burst through his dental-floss bonds and leaped to his hindpaws, then pulled Glory up beside him and started to untie her as well.

Gorgonzola loomed into view. 'Ten centimetres of breakfast, you mean,' he growled.

With him was Muenster Alexanderplatz. The German rat licked his lips. Gorgonzola's stomach growled. As the two hungry rats advanced, Glory and Bunsen shrank back, but there was nowhere to go. The two mice teetered on the brink of the deck's edge, cornered.

Dupont and Brie closed in behind the two mousivores. 'Going some place, short-tails?' sneered Dupont.

Bunsen pulled Glory up beside him. 'Do you trust me?' he whispered.

'Huh?' said Glory, unable to tear her eyes off the rats, especially Brie. The Parisian she-rat was obviously in Coco Chanel mode again, mentally sizing her up for some horrible rat garment.

'Do you trust me?' the lab mouse repeated urgently.

Glory looked at him. 'With all my heart.'

Bunsen reached up, plucked something from his backpack and buckled it round his waist. Then he clasped Glory tightly to him and dived off the side of the balloon.

'Hey!' screeched an astounded Dupont.

'*Zut alors*, my slippers!' cried Brie.

Gorgonzola and Muenster rushed forward and, as she and Bunsen dropped towards the sea like a pair of stones, Glory caught sight of their snouts jutting over the edge of the deck, snarling in frustrated hunger.

'Bunsen! What are you doing!' screamed Glory, her eyes wide with terror.

'Don't look down!' Bunsen reached a paw over his shoulder and pressed something on the gizmo he'd strapped to himself. There was a loud 'HISSSSSSS' and suddenly their flight was arrested. The two mice hung suspended in mid-air for a moment, long enough for Bunsen to pass a strap around Glory and fasten her securely to his utility belt. Then he pressed another button and they shot straight back up towards the *Mayflower*.

'EEEEEEEOOOOOOOOOWWWWWWWW!' cried Glory as they skyrocketed past the ship. 'What the heck is this thing?'

'My latest invention,' Bunsen told her. 'An experimental jet pack. I haven't worked all the bugs out yet.'

Glory craned her neck to peer over the lab mouse's shoulder. Bunsen was wearing what looked like a kazoo. Twin nozzles (foraged from a hair-salon skip, they were attached to trial-size cans of hair spray) stuck out of the bottom like dual exhaust pipes. 'Bunsen,' she said, 'you never cease to amaze me.'

243

Her colleague grinned. 'That's the nicest thing you've ever said to me,' he replied. 'I mean, besides what you said earlier. You know, about me being the only mouse for you and all.'

Bunsen manoeuvred the kazoo-rocket over the *Mayflower*, until the two of them were just a metre above the rats. Glory waggled her paw at Dupont. The Sewer Lord stared up at the two of them, livid with rage.

'You haven't seen the last of me!' he cried, thrashing his tail. 'I'll make mousemeat of you yet!'

'Mousemeat?' Bunsen replied. 'Look around you, Dupont. In a few hours, when that balloon starts to deflate, you'll be nothing but shark-meat.'

The delegates of the Global Rodent Roundtable stirred uneasily.

'Even if it doesn't, it's a long, cold ride to wherever you're going,' added Glory.

'A long ride! What are we going to eat?' one of the rats wailed.

Gorgonzola waddled forward. He pointed to Fumble. 'Antipasto,' he growled.

Six dozen pairs of red rat eyes swivelled towards the stout grey mouse. Fumble quailed.

'What was that about Minister of Mouse Affairs?'

cried Glory. 'Minister of In-flight Meals is more like it! GRR!'

And with that, Bunsen aimed them towards the shore and the two mice flew off, leaving the shipful of hungry rats – and one turn-tail of a mouse – far behind.

They flew onwards in companionable silence, the only sound the gentle hiss from the kazoo's hairspray-powered engine. Soon, the *Mayflower* was a distant speck on the horizon. As the skyline of Manhattan grew closer, Glory felt herself finally relax.

All of a sudden the kazoo started to splutter.

'Uh-oh,' said Bunsen.

Glory stiffened in alarm. 'What?'

'Um, we might be out of fuel. I've only tested this short-distance.'

As the kazoo-rocket sputtered and coughed and finally died, Glory looked down at the water below them. 'Good thing I can swim,' she said bravely.

'One more trick in my bag,' said Bunsen, tugging on his backpack yet again. A small parachute (made from a foraged dinner napkin) blossomed above them, slowing their rapid descent. 'At least it will be a soft landing.'

'I'm sorry I got you into this!' said Glory. 'Me and my stupid pride!'

'I can think of worse things than spending my last moments with the mouse that I, uh – the mouse that I, uh –' Bunsen hesitated. He drew a deep breath. What was he waiting for? It was now or never. 'The mouse that I love,' he finished firmly.

'Oh, Bunsen, I love you too!' cried Glory, her bright little eyes brimming with tears. 'I'm just so sorry that it has to end this way!'

A large shadow swept over them, and the two mice looked up to see a seagull hovering just above their parachute. A familiar face poked over the edge of its wings.

'Care for a lift?' said Squeak Savoy.

At her side was Bubble. He saluted briskly. 'Would hardly be proper to leave you hanging like this,' he added, as the seagull swooped beneath Glory and Bunsen and caught them on its broad back.

'Thanks,' said Glory.

'We owe you one, remember?' said Squeak. 'You saved our tails at Grand Central Station. Bubble and I thought it only fair to return the favour.'

'How did you talk him into it?' asked Bunsen, waving his paw at the seagull. Unlike pigeons, seagulls were notoriously unpredictable. Previous attempts to train them for spy mice missions had not been successful.

Bubble held up a piece of pumpkin chocolate-chip bread. 'Bribery,' he said simply. 'Highly effective in our line of work, I've found.'

The four of them watched as the *Mayflower* disappeared over the horizon.

'Good riddance to bad rubbish,' said Bunsen.

'Bad rodents, don't you mean?' quipped Glory. 'And speaking of rodents, what about Fumble?'

Squeak consulted a tiny compass that hung from her utility belt. 'If the wind holds, we should be able to pick him up on the other side of the pond,' she reported. 'That ship's on a direct course for England.'

'If he survives the trip,' said Bunsen. 'Last we saw of him, he was on his way to becoming an appetizer.'

'Or a pair of slippers,' added Glory. 'Or both.'

Bubble shook his head. 'I highly doubt it. Dupont will never allow it. The information he possesses is far too valuable.'

'Well, he'd only be getting what he deserves,' said Glory, who was not at all regretful at the thought of her turn-tail colleague ending up as a rat snack. She shaded her eyes with her paw and gazed across the harbour. 'Why don't you drop us off there,' she suggested, pointing to the Statue of Liberty. 'It's close enough to shore for us to flag down a Pigeon Air taxi, and that way you can go straight to the airport.'

'Splendid idea,' Bubble replied. He held out another piece of pumpkin chocolate-chip bread for the seagull, and a short time later they landed on top of Lady Liberty's torch.

'Do come and visit us sometime,' said Bubble, as Glory and Bunsen climbed down from the bird's broad back. 'You'd be most welcome in London, and I know Sir Edmund Hazelnut-Cadbury is eager to meet you.'

The two spy mice waved as the seagull bearing their British friends rose into the air.

'Cheerio, then, and good luck!' called Squeak.

'Cheerio!' echoed Glory. She turned to Bunsen and smiled. 'Let's go home.'

CHAPTER
THIRTY-TWO

DAY THREE – THURSDAY 1800 HOURS

'You should have seen their faces!' said Lavinia Levinson. 'Fifteen metres tall on every billboard in Times Square, plastered in pigeon poo.'

DB gave a snort of laughter, and Oz grinned at the recollection. He could smile, now that he knew Glory and Bunsen were safe. B-Nut had sent them a message via pigeon post as soon as he got the news. Vinnie had reached them just before they left the Waldorf-Astoria to return home to Washington.

'I got it all on film, too,' added Amelia Bean proudly. 'A real scoop for Channel Twelve.'

'A scoop of poo,' quipped DB's father, and everyone laughed.

'I say it serves them right, the rascals,' Luigi

Levinson said. 'They had no business picking on our little sugarplums.'

He glanced fondly across the table at Oz and DB. Both families were gathered around the Levinsons' long dinner table for a celebratory Thanksgiving feast. Oz's father had been busy all day preparing for their triumphant return from New York. Turkey, stuffing, mashed potatoes and gravy, sweet-potato casserole with miniature marshmallows – all of Oz's favourites. And pumpkin chocolate-chip bread, of course.

Just then the doorbell rang. Oz's father excused himself to answer it. He returned a moment later with a puzzled look on his face.

'Who was it?' asked Oz's mother.

Luigi Levinson shrugged. 'I don't know,' he replied. 'There was no one there. Just a pigeon on the railing. But this was on the doorstep.'

He handed a small package to Oz. The names 'Ozymandias Levinson and Delilah Bean' were inscribed on the brown-paper wrapping in very precise, very tiny handwriting.

'Looks like our two Bake-off celebrities already have some fans.'

'Pretty soon they'll be asking for your autograph

instead of mine,' added Oz's mother, winking at Amelia Bean.

DB's mother leaned over and inspected the package curiously. 'You almost need a magnifying glass to read that address.'

'Uh, can we be excused?' asked Oz, kicking DB under the table.

'Hey!' cried his friend, scowling. 'What did you – oh. I mean yeah, can we be excused?'

'Certainly,' said Luigi Levinson. 'Clear your places first, please.'

Oz and DB carried their dishes to the kitchen, then ran up to Oz's room. Oz rummaged in his desk for a pair of scissors. He clipped the string and together he and DB unwrapped the package.

'Wow!' breathed Oz.

Inside were a pair of lolly-stick skateboards painted with silver fingernail polish.

'Oz!' said DB, gazing at them in wonder. 'Does this mean what I think it means?'

Oz steered the tiny skateboard around the top of his desk with a pudgy finger. There was a dreamy look in his eye. Even James Bond didn't have one of these. 'I think so,' he replied. He poked through the small box and emerged with a tiny envelope. 'Let's see what the note says.'

It was in code. DB got the magnifying glass while Oz fished the cipher wheel from his pocket. Together they decoded the message.

'FOR YOUR PAWS ONLY', it began. 'IN RECOGNITION OF ANOTHER GOOD JOB WELL DONE, WE AT THE SPY MICE AGENCY HEREBY EXTEND OUR DEEPEST THANKS, AND PROMOTE YOU TO HONORARY SILVER SKATEBOARD STATUS. THE WORLD IS YOURS.' It was signed *Julius Folger.*

'What does he mean, the world is yours?' asked DB, staring at the piece of paper.

'Glory says that the Silver Skateboard agents get all the glamorous overseas postings,' Oz explained.

DB grunted. 'Yeah, right,' she said. 'Chester B. Arthur Elementary is about as glamorous as we get.'

Oz poked at his glasses, then popped a wheelie on his desk with his new lolly-stick skateboard. 'Well, we did get to go to New York, remember?'

'That's true,' DB replied.

'So you never know,' said Oz. 'You just never know.'

CHAPTER
THIRTY-THREE

DAY THREE – THURSDAY 1800 HOURS

'You look fine, Bunsen,' said Glory. 'Relax.'

Across the street from the Levinsons' townhouse, the two mice were standing on the doorstep of the giant oak tree where the Goldenleaf family lived. Bunsen fidgeted nervously with his bow tie.

'Are you sure I have it on straight?' he squeaked, his nose and tail an anxious pink.

Glory plucked a small brass key from a pocket on her backpack and

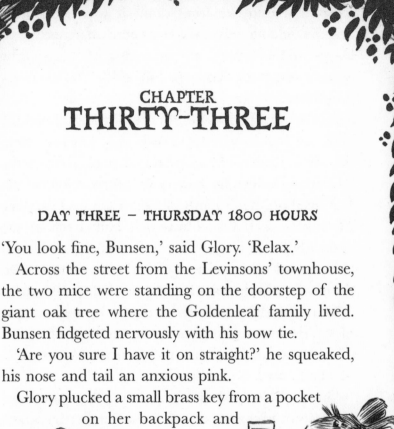

inserted it into her front door. It was a beautiful door, its elaborately carved pattern of intertwined leaves and acorns a mirror image of the nearby estate's iron gates. 'Trust me,' she said. 'You look very handsome.'

As they stepped inside, Bunsen looked about the entrance hall in wonder. It was very different from the sterile white walls and stainless-steel tables of the laboratory where he had been raised. Goldenleafs had lived on the grounds of Dumbarton Oaks since the big brick mansion was first built back in the early 1800s, and their home reflected nearly two centuries of gracious living. The walls were painted the colour of a ripe peach and the oak floor, its honey-coloured surface polished smooth by generations of Goldenleaf paws, gleamed in the light of a pair of birthday candles that flickered from paper-clip sconces.

'Snug, isn't it?' asked Glory, sliding her skateboard into its slot in the cupboard. She hung her backpack neatly on its peg above the plumply upholstered bench and led the way upstairs.

As they climbed the staircase that wound through the heart of the tree, Glory lifted her elegant little nose and sniffed the air. 'Mmmm mmmm,' she said.

'A real Thanksgiving feast!' She sighed a deep, contented sigh.

'Do you really think they'll like me?' fretted Bunsen, as the sound of conversation and laughter drew closer.

Glory paused. She turned and looked down on him from the stair above, then leaned over impulsively and kissed the tip of his nose. 'What's not to like?' she replied with a saucy wink.

Upstairs, they found the Goldenleaf family seated round a long, narrow table (a domino box foraged from the nearby mansion's attic long ago) covered with crisp white linen. At one end was Glory's distinguished field-mouse father, General Dumbarton Goldenleaf; at the other sat Glory's mother, Gingersnap Goldenleaf, a pleasantly round grey house mouse with a particularly attractive set of whiskers. Julius Folger was seated to her right. Hotspur was nowhere to be seen. Rumour had it that his uncle had sent him packing. Posted to a desk job in Nome, Alaska, to cool his tail for a bit and reflect on his reckless decision that had nearly cost two spy mice – not to mention several humans – their lives.

Ringing the rest of the table were Glory's sixteen brothers and sisters. Perched in matchbox high chairs

255

near their mother were Truffle and Taffy, the babies (or candy batch, as they were called, for in honour of her Bakery Guild roots Gingersnap Goldenleaf had given all her children names that reflected their house-mouse heritage).

Further down, where their father could keep an eye on them, were the school-age 'cookies' – Snickerdoodle, Macaroon, Hermit and Brownie. Seated around them were the French pastries: Croissant, Éclair, Petit Four, Napoleon and Chantilly. The oldest batch of Goldenleaf offspring, they had moved out last year and were already launched on lives of their own. Soon, Glory knew, it would be her turn to leave the nest and make her way in the world, but for now she was perfectly happy living here at home.

A shout of laughter went up around the room as B-Nut finished describing the aerial pigeon bombing of Jordan and Tank in Times Square.

'You should have seen their faces when they saw themselves on the billboards!' he said with glee. 'A real pair of great white sharks!'

Gingersnap Goldenleaf looked over towards the doorway. 'Glory!' she cried in delight. 'You're home!' She sprang up from the table and scampered over to hug her daughter. 'Shove over,' she said to the 'muffins' (who in addition to B-Nut and Glory included their batchmates Chip, Bran, Pumpkin and Blueberry). 'Make room for our guests of honour.'

She turned to Bunsen. 'You must be Glory's beau!' she said, enveloping the lab mouse in a warm hug, too. 'I've heard so much about you, Mr Burner.'

'You have?' squeaked Bunsen in surprise.

'Certainly,' said Gingersnap, shooting her husband a significant look. 'Haven't we, dear?'

'Uh, yes, of course. Absolutely. Quite right. Glory talks of little else.' General Goldenleaf stood up, extending his paw. 'Good to see you again, Bunsen. I understand from B-Nut here that we owe our daughter's life to you once more.'

'Well, I, uh, that is –' Bunsen stammered.

'C'mon, Bunsen, admit it,' said B-Nut. 'You're a hero!'

'I don't know about that,' replied the lab mouse. 'Glory helped, too. And don't forget Bubble and Squeak.'

'Who are Bubble and Squeak?' piped Snicker-doodle.

Julius winked at him. 'That's "For Your Paws Only",' he whispered. 'Top Secret.' He lifted his cider cup in a toast. 'Here's to the many brave mice in this room, and to all their colleagues!'

'Especially Bunsen,' said Glory, reaching over and clasping the lab mouse's pale paw in her own soft brown one. 'He's true blue. And far too modest.' She took a seat beside Julius.

'So glad to see you home safe and sound, my dear,' said the elder mouse. 'And hearty congratulations for disposing so neatly of Dupont. Not to mention all the rest of the Global Rodent Roundtable.'

Glory frowned. She wasn't so sure that Roquefort Dupont wouldn't turn up again. He had more lives than a cat. Still, no point worrying about it now. Pushing all unpleasant rodent thoughts aside, she surveyed the room with satisfaction. It was painted a warm, glowing cranberry with glossy white trim, and portraits of Goldenleaf ancestors beamed down at them from the walls. A cheery blaze burned in the fireplace, its light joined by the twinkling birthday-candle chandelier overhead. And the table! Glory's mother had outdone herself with the table. It was spread with all of their finest things – bowls made from polished walnut shells, crystal punch cups foraged from an abandoned doll's house a century ago, and at each place one of her family's prized heirlooms gleamed in the candlelight – tiny silver salt spoons plucked from the rubbish by an enterprising Goldenleaf after a careless servant at Dumbarton Oaks had thrown them out.

Bunsen, meanwhile, eyed the bounty. A generous tureen of butternut-squash soup held place of honour in the centre of the table. Surrounding it were platters piled high with golden kernels of corn, yeast rolls, toasted nuts, apple slices and more. On the sideboard, a row of pumpkin pies awaited the dessert course.

'This looks wonderful,' he said happily.

'Please help yourself,' said Gingersnap Goldenleaf, and the feast began.

Glory gazed around the table fondly at her family and friends. She couldn't remember ever feeling more content. She had an adventurous job by day, and a cosy home to return to at night. Best of all, at her side was a fine, brave, loyal mouse who loved her, and whom she loved in return.

I'm the luckiest mouse in the whole wide world, thought Glory.

'Bunsen,' she whispered.

'Mmmm?' replied her colleague. His mouth was full of chestnut stuffing, and he had a blissful expression on his face. Behind them, where no one else could see, his tail was intertwined with hers.

Glory smiled. 'Please pass the cranberry sauce.'